The Heirs of Wishcliffe

Welcome to the world of the English aristocracy...

With aristocracy running through their blood, three men are set to claim their inheritance and their homes, no matter the cost. But when three women walk into their lives, they realize they have more to contend with than they were expecting!

Introducing Toby Blythe, thirteenth Viscount of Wishcliffe. When tragedy strikes his family, he decides his accidental marriage in Vegas could work in his favor upon his return to England...

Meet Lord Finn Clifford, Toby's best friend, healing from a family betrayal. He must track down the lost family heirlooms, but he may have just tracked down his soul mate along the way!

Finally, we meet Max Blythe, Toby's illegitimate half brother, who until now has been making his own luck in life. Perhaps this luck leaves him with more than he bargained for...

Find out what happens in

Toby and Autumn's story
Vegas Wedding to Forever

and

Finn and Victoria's story
Their Second Chance Miracle

and

Max and Lena's story
Baby on the Rebel Heir's Doorstep

Available now from Harlequin Romance!

Dear Reader,

Welcome back to Wishcliffe!

This time, we're in the neighboring village of Wells-on-Water with Max Blythe, the illegitimate son of old Viscount Wishcliffe. Max is trying to start a new life in the village that scorned him growing up—something that's going to get an awful lot more complicated with the arrival of two women in his life. One he knew years ago and walked away from. And one just arrived on his doorstep in a basket, with a note addressed to him...

I've loved writing this Heirs of Wishcliffe series—so much so that I also wrote a free companion story called *Reunited in Wishcliffe*! If you're not ready to leave Wishcliffe just yet, you can find it on the Harlequin website or at www.sophiepembroke.com.

Love and confetti,

Sophie x

Baby on the Rebel Heir's Doorstep

Sophie Pembroke

Recycling programs for this product may not exist in your area.

ISBN-13: 978-1-335-73676-5

Baby on the Rebel Heir's Doorstep

For questions and comments about the quality of this book, please contact us at CustomerService@Harlequin.com.

Harlequin Enterprises ULC
22 Adelaide St. West, 41st Floor
Toronto, Ontario M5H 4E3, Canada
www.Harlequin.com

Printed in U.S.A.

Sophie Pembroke has been dreaming, reading and writing romance ever since she read her first Harlequin novel as part of her English literature degree at Lancaster University, so getting to write romantic fiction for a living really is a dream come true! Born in Abu Dhabi, Sophie grew up in Wales and now lives in a little Hertfordshire market town with her scientist husband, her incredibly imaginative and creative daughter, and her adventurous, adorable little boy. In Sophie's world, happy *is* forever after, everything stops for tea and there's always time for one more page...

Books by Sophie Pembroke

Harlequin Romance

The Heirs of Wishcliffe

Vegas Wedding to Forever
Their Second Chance Miracle

Cinderellas in the Spotlight

Awakening His Shy Cinderella
A Midnight Kiss to Seal the Deal

A Fairytale Summer!

Italian Escape with Her Fake Fiancé

Snowbound with the Heir
Second Chance for the Single Mom
The Princess and the Rebel Billionaire

Visit the Author Profile page
at Harlequin.com for more titles.

For everyone who has ever arrived home with a new baby, then wondered what on earth you're supposed to do next…(and for the next eighteen years!).

Praise for Sophie Pembroke

"An emotionally satisfying contemporary romance full of hope and heart, *Second Chance for the Single Mom* is the latest spellbinding tale from Sophie Pembroke's very gifted pen. A poignant and feel-good tale that touches the heart and lifts the spirits."

—*Goodreads*

CHAPTER ONE

THE BALLROOM AT Clifford House was packed, wall to wall, with the great and good of local society. Lena Phillips glanced around the busy room and took in the familiar faces. Hmm. Also the less great and notoriously *not* so good, too, by her assessment. Although, in places as small as Wells-on-Water and Wishcliffe, she supposed hosts couldn't afford to be too stingy with the invitation list if they wanted a full house.

But it did mean her brothers were likely to be in attendance. Neither Gary nor Keith were ones to miss a free drink or a party, and she didn't believe for a moment that either of them would have been responsible enough to stay back and take care of The Fox, the family pub their father had left them when he died, two years ago.

She was almost surprised they hadn't asked her to cover for them. Perhaps after months of refusing to listen to any of her ideas on how to improve the place they'd assumed—correctly—

that she'd turn them down flat. In the past, she wouldn't have. She'd never wanted to let her father down. But she had no such concerns about Gary and Keith. Well, hardly any.

She was worried about The Fox, though…

Helping herself to a glass of champagne from a passing waiter's tray—just one, she still had to drive home later—Lena scanned the room again and began mentally cataloguing who she needed to speak to tonight, and in what order. She could see the Reverend Dominic Spade across the way by the terrace; she should collar him about holding the food bank at the church over the summer holidays, at least. But first she needed to speak to Trevor and Kathy about the news of the sale of the village hall and what it meant for their community hub. And she should probably try and find Paul Gardiner, the local estate agent, before that. See what information she could pry out of him…

Across the room she could see the party's hostess, Victoria Blythe—soon to be Clifford—mingling, a smile on her face, her hands resting on her pregnant belly. It was good to see; after the terrible loss of her husband and only son, Lena hadn't been sure that her friend would ever smile again. But it seemed that Finn Clifford had found a way to make her future bright.

She'd catch Victoria later, though. First she had village matters to attend to.

She couldn't spot Paul, and Rev Spade was standing a little too close to where Gary and Keith were holding court on the terrace for her liking, so Lena headed for the buffet table and Trevor and Kathy instead.

'Ah, Lena! Just the person I was looking for,' Trevor said as she joined them.

'You weren't looking for anything beyond the next of those mini sausage rolls.' Kathy snatched one of them from his plate and popped it in her mouth before he could object. 'You look lovely tonight, love.'

Lena glanced down at her shimmering blue dress, smoothing the fabric again over her hips, where it clung tight before falling all the way to the ground over her silver heels. 'Thanks.'

The mystery of Trevor and Kathy was one Lena had never quite managed to solve, despite having known them both pretty much all her life. They weren't married, that much was certain—she'd checked the parish records to be sure—and they didn't live together, either. Instead, they occupied two adjoining terrace houses in a side street not far from the pub where Lena grew up, and were both regulars.

She'd never seen anything to suggest a romantic relationship between them, and they bickered far too much to be actual friends… and yet, they were nearly always seen together.

One day she'd figure it out. But today she had other priorities.

'I was looking for you two as well.' She eyed the buffet table. 'And maybe those duck spring rolls.'

Kathy grabbed her a plate, added several spring rolls, two sausage rolls, and a chicken satay skewer, then handed it over. 'Do you have news?'

Lena shook her head. 'I was sort of hoping you would. Nothing on the Save The Village Hall petition, then?'

'Apparently our "esteemed" local councillor has been telling everyone he speaks to that the hall was falling apart, and there was no money to repair the roof after it caved in, so selling it is the only option.' The expression on Trevor's face told Lena exactly what he thought of Councillor Morgan. She didn't entirely disagree.

'The biggest problem is that he's right.' Kathy sighed. 'The estimates on replacing the roof alone were astronomical, and it just wasn't getting enough use to warrant it. Even the local Brownies group decided to use the school hall instead, after the last storm. Brown Owl said there were more buckets than girls in there.'

'So they're just going to sell it for housing, like everything else around here.' The old cinema in Wishcliffe had been demolished and turned into flats five years ago, and even the Wells-on-Water Methodist chapel was now a *Grand Designs* transformation in progress.

'That's the talk,' Trevor confirmed, his voice glum.

'On the bright side, though, it looks like some of the money from the sale will go into the community funds account we set up as part of the charitable trust thing for the hall.' Kathy's face brightened as she spoke. 'So once it all goes through, we can start looking for a new location for the community hub project again.'

'That's good,' Lena said, although she couldn't quite find the same enthusiasm as Kathy. Whatever money they raised from the sale of the hall, it was unlikely to be enough to buy and pay for the upkeep of another property. Which meant renting, which would deplete funds even faster. She foresaw a lot of fundraising in her future.

Good thing that one of her main talents was sweet-talking the rich and privileged into supporting community projects. Well, that and running pubs. She was a woman of many talents, really—all of them unappreciated by her family.

But when something mattered to her, she didn't give up. And this village—and its people—mattered. So she'd find a way, as she always did.

'What we really need is a sponsor,' Trevor mused. 'Someone with the money and the inclination—or guilt… I'd take guilt—to make them want to do good deeds.'

'Guilt is very motivating,' Kathy agreed. Lena looked down at her plate and refused to think about her own motives. 'What about Finn Clifford, since we're here? Think we could hit him up for some contributions?'

'Probably,' Lena said, looking up to scan the room again in search of likely targets. 'But he's only just moved back here and he's got the baby on the way and the wedding to plan. We might get some money, but he's not going to be a figurehead or get properly involved or anything.'

'Besides, he's out here at Clifford House,' Trevor pointed out. 'Closer to Wishcliffe than Wells-on-Water. And for the community hub to be a success, we really do need someone connected to our community, don't we?'

Kathy hummed her agreement as, across the room, another figure caught Lena's eye, talking with their hostess. A tall, dark, brooding sort of a figure, he stuck out in the ballroom like a cactus in a rose garden. A large, prickly, unwelcome cactus.

He looks like…

The man turned, and Lena got a good look at his face, her eyes widening with recognition.

Never mind looked like. It *was*.

Even if she hadn't recognised his face, the

way her heart suddenly beat double time would have given it away.

Quickly, she spun away, facing the buffet table again, suddenly very, very interested in the miniature Yorkshire puds with beef and horseradish.

But Kathy had already followed her gaze, it seemed. 'Now, there's a thought. Max Blythe. He's just inherited the Manor House, hasn't he? That's *definitely* Wells-on-Water territory, and by all accounts he's absolutely loaded. What do you think, Lena?'

I think if I never talk to Max Blythe again it'll be too soon.

'Perhaps,' Lena said, non-committally, trying to keep all the memories buried deep in her chest. 'What do you think about the halloumi fries? Too greasy?'

Kathy and Trevor ignored her attempts at canapé-based conversation.

'Heads up, ladies,' Trevor said. 'Victoria's got him in her grasp now. And they're heading this way.'

Max Blythe hated parties.

As a rule, he wasn't all that fond of gatherings, shindigs or social get-togethers in general. But he really didn't like parties.

Even ones as deliciously catered and with

such good libations as the one Finn and Victoria were throwing tonight.

His problem wasn't with his hosts, who seemed like perfectly nice and reasonable people. It wasn't even that they'd invited him there tonight since it seemed they'd invited *everyone* in the vicinity and that now, rather unexpectedly, included him.

No, Max's issue with tonight's party in particular was the Looks.

He didn't think there was a single attendee not guilty of giving him one—unless, somehow, they hadn't spotted him yet. A few people had tried to talk to him—or, more likely, get some gossip out of him—but they'd all been easily rebuffed. The rest...they just looked.

They said more with a Look than they could with words, though. In every Look Max read a maelstrom of thoughts and emotions.

Curiosity, of course, about why he'd returned to Wells-on-Water after so many years, and about what his relationship with the Blythe family was now. Resentment or disappointment from many who'd known him as a child. Pity from some, probably those remembering his mother. Anger from others, seeing where he'd managed to take his life. Appreciation, from some female gazes—but that, at least, was familiar from other settings, much as he tended to ignore it. The fascination with his family, his history—that was all particular to this area of the country. Wishcliffe and Wells-on-Water, the neighbouring small town and village by the sea that had witnessed his miserable childhood. The same place he'd vowed never to return to after his mother's death.

Until Toby Blythe, Viscount Wishcliffe, had changed all that.

Max wasn't entirely sure how much his half-brother had made known to the general population of the area about his existence and why Toby had gifted him the Manor House at Wells-on-Water, but in his experience very little stayed secret in a place like Wishcliffe. And it wasn't as if anyone who'd lived in the area while he was growing up could have missed the pointed way his mother had named him Blythe, even if his father had never acknowledged him.

It was an open secret—and humiliation—in the community. Max was the illegitimate son of the old viscount, born between the two legitimate heirs, Barnaby and Toby. His mother had never tried to hide who he was, never denied it—in fact, she'd seemed to revel in forcing the uncomfortable truth on everyone.

You have to do what's right in this world, Max, even when it's hard, she'd always said. *And when it feels hardest, that's when it matters most.*

And it *had* been hard. His whole childhood, it had been unbearably hard. Dealing with all the sniggers behind his back that turned to all-out bullying as he grew older. The disapproving looks from the adults in the village, probably aimed more at his mother for 'flaunting her sin'—as one of them had put it once—than at him, but which still made him feel like a disappointment just for existing. And seeing, every single day, that huge house on the hill and knowing his father was up there with his two half-brothers, all pretending he didn't exist.

Was it any wonder he'd rebelled? Caused the kind of trouble that *made* people pay attention to him, rather than try to ignore his existence? That lived down to their every expectation of it?

Or that he'd run away as fast and as far as he could, as soon as sixth form was over?

He'd headed out into a world who didn't know or care who he was, and showed them who he could be without all that baggage hanging over him. He'd kept the surname—what else would he call himself after so long?—but outside Wishcliffe and Wells-on-Water the name Blythe didn't mean a damn thing to anyone. It was wonderfully freeing.

He'd made his fortune, made his own name, made his own life. And he'd been happy with it.

Until an email from Toby had turned everything upside down.

Now, here he was, back in the heart of Wishcliffe society, staring down all the looks and the disappointment again. Except, this time, he was there as Toby Blythe's brother. Rightful heir of the Manor House above Wells-on-Water village. His father might never have acknowledged him in his lifetime, but the old viscount's son had.

Max *belonged* now. Even if he still wasn't a hundred per cent sure he wanted to.

Not if it meant attending parties like this all the time, anyway.

'They'll get used to you soon enough,' Toby had said, when he and his new wife Autumn had invited Max to dinner the previous weekend. *'Forget you ever went away.'*

But Max didn't want them to forget. He wanted them to remember everything he'd achieved *in spite* of being the illegitimate son of Viscount Wishcliffe.

And more than anything, he didn't want anybody remembering the pathetic, lost and lonely boy he'd been before he moved away.

A movement across the room caught his eye—mostly because it was moving towards him. He steeled himself for another encounter with a local looking for gossip, before realising that it was actually his hostess approaching him.

Victoria Blythe made her way across the ballroom, her ever-growing belly clearing a path before her. Max couldn't help but smile; he'd met Victoria and her fiancé, Finn Clifford, at the Sunday dinner at Wishcliffe the weekend before and found his elder half-brother's widow to be both insightful and determined. Which was how she'd persuaded him to attend tonight in the first place.

'Max, they're going to talk about you whatever you do,' she'd said. *'At least if you're there it's harder for them to do it behind your back.'*

'Victoria,' Max said as she reached him. 'Thank you for inviting me tonight. You have a lovely home.' That sounded like the right sort of thing to say, didn't it?

She inclined her head to accept the compliment, so he assumed it was. 'Thank you for coming. I'm sorry my home is filled with such gossips.'

He chuckled at that, which made her smile.

'Why don't I find someone to introduce you to who probably won't ask you too many invasive questions?' she suggested.

'That would be nice,' Max replied cautiously, unsure that there *was* anyone in the room who wouldn't. But he couldn't exactly say, 'I'm happier standing here glaring at all your guests, thanks,' could he?

Victoria scanned the room for a moment, and then smiled in a way that made Max even more nervous.

'Perfect.' Taking Max's arm, she led him towards her target, as he wondered if there was still time to make a run for the door.

Then he realised exactly who Victoria was taking him to, and decided that diving out of the window would probably suffice. Anything except talking to—

But it was too late.

The blonde ahead of them, the one in the shimmering blue dress that clung to curves he remembered well, was already turning to face them. The older couple she was talking to began to fade backwards into the crowd around the buffet table, smiles on their lips.

'Max, let me introduce Lena Phillips. She's the manager of the King's Arms pub in Wishcliffe.'

Lena raised perfectly arched eyebrows in surprise, every inch the perfect class princess she'd been at school. 'Max Blythe. Really.'

Really what? Really there? Really daring to speak to her again? Really assuming she'd want to talk to him after their last…interaction, the night before he skipped town?

Max wasn't sure. So he just said, 'Apparently so. Hello, Lena.'

* * *

There wasn't much for it other than to brazen it out, Lena decided. Trevor and Kathy were already moving away towards the desserts table—traitors—and leaving her alone to face her doom. They probably assumed she'd be sweet-talking Max Blythe into donating squillions to set up some state-of-the-art community hub centre complete with computer access for those without it and a coffee shop with a ready supply of sausage rolls. When actually, she would just be trying to get the hell away from him as soon as possible.

Which would be easier if Victoria weren't standing right there watching them.

She needed to say something, Lena realised. Continue an actual normal conversation like normal people.

As if the last time she'd seen Max Blythe hadn't been minutes after he took her virginity in the back of his beaten-up car, then skipped town without looking back. As if that one night hadn't changed the trajectory of her whole life.

At least he looked as shell-shocked at the unexpected reunion as she felt. He deserved to feel awkward and embarrassed. She didn't. *He* was the one who'd run out, after all. Well, run *first* anyway.

Victoria opened her mouth, obviously about

to fill the uncomfortable silence, but before she could speak her fiancé, Finn, appeared at her side.

'Excuse me, Max, Lena, I just need to borrow my fiancée for a moment.'

'Borrow me?' Lena heard Victoria object as he steered her out of the ballroom. 'What am I? A phone charger?'

And then it was just her and Max. For the first time in sixteen years, since they were both eighteen and stupid.

'I didn't realise you'd be here tonight,' Lena said, not adding that she might not have attended herself if she had done. He'd guess that part, and it wasn't true, anyway. She'd have come—not to see him, but because of the networking opportunities Victoria's party offered. Because her life had nothing to do with him any more.

Lena hoped he got all that from her short, unimaginative statement.

Max gave her a crooked smile. 'You might be the only one here who didn't, then. Seems to me that the primary reason for attendance for most people was to stare awkwardly at me.'

'I think you'll find it was actually the sausage rolls,' Lena countered. 'They're surprisingly good.'

And you're not actually the centre of anyone's world, Max Blythe.

So many things she wanted to say to him.

Curses and accusations and cutting remarks. Explanations and apologies, and the secrets she'd held tight to her chest for so long. But she wasn't eighteen any more. At thirty-four, she'd learned to hold her tongue. To make nice, build bridges, charm people. Everything she needed to do for her business, and for her work in the community.

What she needed to do to make Wells-on-Water a better place. A place that eighteen-year-olds like they'd been didn't need to run away from in the first place.

But right now she wished she could be that young and careless again. A girl who hadn't learned to be so nice, yet. One who still said what she was really thinking.

Oh, who was she kidding? She'd never been that girl. Ever since her mother died when she was young, Lena had learned to say whatever she needed to say to keep everyone happy, to secure her place in the community, even if she was the daughter of a drunk and sister to two of the biggest troublemakers in the village.

'Sausage rolls?' Max looked hopefully over at the buffet table, just as Trevor popped the last one into his mouth.

Lena shrugged, feeling childishly pleased. 'You can't hang around at these things. You miss your chance and those sausage rolls are gone for ever.'

'I guess I'll have to wait for the next party,' Max replied, and Lena felt a jolt of uncertainty go through her.

'You're planning on staying around this time, then?' She cursed the words the moment they were out of her mouth. *Why* did she have to make reference to the *last* time they'd spoken? She'd wanted to pretend it had never happened at all. Or that if it had, she hadn't thought about it since. Now that was blown out of the water.

And she could tell from the surprise in Max's eyes, and the slow smile that followed, that he knew exactly what she'd been thinking about.

'Well,' he said, slowly, 'Toby did give me an entire house. Seems a shame to waste it.'

Since the house in question was closer to a mansion, Lena couldn't exactly disagree. Which didn't mean she wouldn't try.

'I'm just surprised you'd want it,' she said. 'I seem to remember you being quite adamant about getting the hell out of Wells-on-Water, and Wishcliffe, and never coming back.'

'That was a long time ago,' Max replied. 'I like to think I've grown up a bit since then.'

And boy, had he. The Max she remembered at eighteen had been darkly handsome, with the same dark brown eyes under his black hair, but he hadn't been *built* like the man in front of her was. At eighteen he'd been lanky and gorgeous, but Max Blythe at thirty-four looked… dangerous. From the broad, broad shoulders to the way his chest filled out his dinner jacket, and how those golden-brown eyes glittered with more than just a promise tonight. Tonight, they held knowledge of the world, and a cynicism that even Max at eighteen hadn't been able to match.

In short, he'd grown up. And he'd grown up *well.*

Of course, Lena liked to think she had, too. She might not be quite the perky blonde teenager he'd left behind, but she'd replaced that youthful enthusiasm with plenty of things she valued more. Self-knowledge, for one. And a daily yoga routine that kept her both toned *and* less stressed.

'We've all grown up,' she murmured, and watched as that dark gaze scanned the length of her, from her highlighted hair to the high heels on her feet, taking in the carefully chosen dress on the way. She looked good tonight and, seeing Max again, she was damn pleased she'd made the effort.

Except she always made the effort, and she made it for herself, not for him or anyone else.

She could feel the tension, the attraction, shimmering between them, the same way it had that last night. Then, it had been a shock—something utterly unexpected. Now, it felt different. Part familiar, inevitable even. But part new, because they weren't eighteen-year-old innocents any longer.

Now, they both knew what the deal was. What they could have, if they wanted it.

She met his gaze, and knew that Max felt it too.

Then his attention jerked away, to something happening behind her. Lena glanced back over her shoulder and suppressed a groan at the sight of her two brothers trying to toss profiteroles into each other's mouths.

'Well, most of us have grown up,' Max amended, and with a wince, Lena nodded her agreement.

'I should probably…' She trailed off with a vague wave towards Gary and Kevin. Typical that they'd ruin the first interesting interaction she'd had with a man in years.

Max raised one eyebrow. 'Why? They're adults, aren't they? Not your responsibility.'

'Maybe not. But—' But what? He was right, damn him. They *weren't* her responsibility, even with both their parents gone. Hell, they were even older than she was. And yet, she knew that everyone in this room would expect her to step in, hand them both some coffee, and keep them out of trouble until they sobered up. Just as she had every other time in living memory.

God, she was sick of it.

Taking care of the community was one thing. Being responsible for her feckless, thoughtless and immature brothers was another.

'I say, leave them to it and come out onto the terrace with me, where we can have a proper catch-up. I mean, it's been a long time, Lena. I'd love to hear what you've been up to.'

Oh, this was exactly how he'd got her into that car sixteen years ago. That hint of a promise in his voice, the one that offered to take her away from all the things about her life that drove her crazy.

And she'd fallen for it, and then he'd left. And she'd been alone for everything that came next.

But this time…this time she was an adult. In charge of her own life. She could leave any time she wanted. And all he was suggesting was a conversation on the terrace, where she didn't have to watch her idiot brothers embarrass themselves—and, by proxy, her. If she wanted it to lead anywhere else…it would be up to her.

'Okay,' she said, and he smiled as she headed for the door, knowing he would follow.

Just a conversation. And this time, it would be Lena who walked away at the end of it. Or didn't.

CHAPTER TWO

OF ALL THE people Max had expected to reconnect with on his return home, Lena Phillips hadn't been one of them. Oh, not because he'd forgotten about her, or because he'd hoped to avoid her. He just simply hadn't imagined for a moment that she'd still be there.

She'd always claimed that she loved Wells-on-Water too much to leave, had told him so even that last night they'd spent together. But she'd also always shone so bright, so vibrant, he'd just assumed there would be some more exciting future out there for her somewhere.

And now he had an opportunity to find out why she'd never left, the way he had.

He pushed the terrace door shut behind them, hoping for a tiny bit of privacy, although glancing along the stone space outside the row of glass doors, all open to the ballroom, that seemed unlikely. The warm summer evening air had tempted plenty of other partygoers out onto the terrace, where they lingered by the sweet flowering roses that climbed the stone latticework between the gardens and the house. But there was enough clear space between their dark corner and the crowds that Max felt confident they should be able to speak in relative privacy.

But Lena was already looking back through the glass into the ballroom at the clownish antics of her brothers. That wasn't what he wanted here at all, so Max slipped between her and the door to block her view.

She refocussed on him and smiled—but it was one of those smiles that didn't quite reach her eyes. A sharp, polite, society smile.

He didn't like it.

Lena's smile was something he remembered most from before. She was always smiling at someone or something, always keeping the peace and lightening difficult situations. Even those smiles had felt more real than this one.

But the smile he really wanted to see was one he'd only ever seen once before. That last night, at the party by the river to celebrate the end of sixth form, the end of their official school careers, before everyone left for university or work or whatever life held for them.

The secret smile she'd saved only for him, as they'd left their classmates getting drunk on the riverbank and escaped to the privacy of his new-to-him fourth-hand car…

He'd thought, when he'd spotted Lena across the room, that she was the last person he wanted to see in this place. But remembering that smile, he couldn't help but wonder if she was the *only* person he wanted to see.

'So,' Lena said, that sharp smile still in place. 'You wanted to talk about what's happened over the last sixteen years? Why don't you start? You were heading to London, I seem to recall, the last time we spoke?'

She didn't mention that she'd been half naked in the back seat of his car when he told her that. Curled up in his arms, a summer breeze floating in through the half-open window. The sex had been a little awkward—although still mind-blowing for him, as an eighteen-year-old virgin. But the conversation afterwards had been strangely comfortable, given how little the two of them had talked in the years before.

'London, yeah.' He shook the image of her eighteen-year-old self from his mind and focussed on the grown woman in front of him. 'I moved there, got a job, studied at night, that kind of thing.'

'And you did all right for yourself, by all accounts.'

'I did.' If becoming a millionaire before twenty-five and doubling it every year since counted as doing all right. 'I worked my way up to taking charge of the company I started at, then broke away and began my own firm. It's done well.'

'And now you're back here.' For the first time that evening, he saw genuine curiosity on her face. 'Why on earth would you want to do that? And don't give me that line about having grown up again. I don't believe that you suddenly got nostalgic for this place when you hit your thirties.'

Max barked a laugh at that. 'Maybe not. But…a lot does change in sixteen years.'

'Like your father died.' Had she always been this blunt? He couldn't remember. Maybe.

The Lena Phillips he'd known in school had been popular, pretty and friends with everyone. She'd been head girl, in charge of basically every student event they'd held, and the first on everyone's birthday invite list. And despite all the movie cliches, she'd actually been *liked*.

Even by him.

But she hadn't shied away from the difficult things, and she wasn't now, it seemed.

'Yes. He did,' Max said. 'And my half-brother, Barnaby, too.'

Lena's expression turned sombre. 'You have to know how sorry I was to hear about that.'

Max shrugged. 'It wasn't like I knew him.' The

Blythe brothers—the official ones, anyway—hadn't gone to the local primary and secondary schools as he and Lena had. They'd been sent away to expensive, exclusive boarding schools, with the likes of Finn Clifford. They hadn't needed to make friends in the local area, although Toby had, a little, Max thought. But not with him. Whether that was because his father had warned him away, or just coincidence, because Max was a little older, he'd never quite found the courage to ask.

Still, it was a strange feeling, losing family he'd never really known.

When his mother had died, Max had lost a part of his heart, as if it had been ripped from his chest. And it had ended any real connection he'd had with Wells-on-Water, or Wishcliffe. He hadn't imagined ever finding a reason to return.

Until Toby got in touch.

But learning that his father had died had been different. More like missing a step on the staircase—a jolt, a brief moment where the world seemed to wobble, then snap back to normal as he found his footing again.

Barnaby's death, along with his young son, Harry, in a sailing accident at sea, had hit harder. Because even if his older half-brother had never acknowledged him, and his nephew hadn't known he existed at all, they were still too young. It was still a tragedy.

And a lost opportunity. Any chance that Max might have come to know them, one day, was gone.

Maybe that was why he'd answered Toby's email, when before then he'd have said for sure that he would ignore it.

'*Was* that what made you return?' Lena asked. 'Their deaths, I mean.'

Max knew that every person inside the ballroom tonight had wanted to ask the same question, but only Lena had the guts to actually do it. He wouldn't have answered the question from anybody else.

But Lena…

There was still a lingering guilt that hung over him at odd moments about the way he'd left her that last night. Maybe that was why he felt as if he owed her the truth.

'Partly. Toby…after he became the viscount, he found a letter our father wrote, before his death, telling them about me.' It was the only time, as far as Max was aware, that the old viscount had ever admitted that Max was his son. 'And he got in touch. Asked to meet me. Said he wanted to make things right.'

As if that were possible. As if it weren't all thirty-four years too bloody late.

But Toby had wanted to try. And that had meant something, despite it all.

Maybe it wasn't too late for other things to mean something, too. Like an apology for running out on Lena sixteen years earlier, without ever looking back.

He knew, instinctively, that they'd need to address that night at some point, if he wanted to continue any connection with Lena now he was back in town. And standing in the darkness with her, feeling the frisson of attraction that seemed to spark between them, Max knew he *did* want that. Even if it meant apologising, embarrassingly late after the fact.

He opened his mouth to say sorry, but Lena spoke first. 'So he gave you the Manor House at Wells-on-Water. And all the responsibility that goes with it. Interesting.'

Apologies flew from his mind. 'Responsibility?'

The terror in Max's eyes was honestly quite amusing—even if it had replaced the heat between them that had started to glow there. This party was definitely turning out to be more fun than she'd anticipated.

'Responsibility?' She could almost hear him gulp after the word. 'What responsibility?'

Lena gave a light shrug. 'Oh, you know. The

owners of those old manor houses always have a certain sort of obligation to look after the village they're connected to, don't they?'

'Still?' Max asked. 'I thought that was one of those Middle Ages feudal-system things.'

'Oh, no.' Lena shook her head. Really, this was almost too easy. 'I mean, most of the cottages in Wells-on-Water *belonged* to the Manor House until surprisingly recently. We would all have been your tenants, not so long ago. And you know how our village feels about tradition.'

'Unfortunately.' Was he remembering all the summer fetes and traditional festivals of their youth, or—more likely—the disapproving glances his mother had earned from the more 'traditional' members of their society when he was growing up? Lena suspected the latter.

Really, she'd have thought there was hardly anything *more* traditional in British aristocracy than a son born, as her gran would have said, 'on the wrong side of the bedsheets'.

But it was clearly a sore spot for Max, even now. She should probably stop tormenting him.

Only it was so much fun…

'What, exactly, will the village be expecting me to do, now I've moved in?'

Lena smothered a laugh at the apprehension in Max's voice. 'Oh, you know. Just the usual. There's the summer fete, to be held on the grounds, of course. A few open days through the year to let the locals poke around the Manor House. The harvest festival feast for the workers, of course, and the usual Yuletide celebrations—you have to kick off the carol singing, for definite. Oh, and the New Year's Eve ball, the Easter egg hunt—'

'Where I have to dress up as the Easter bunny?' Max asked, drily.

'Of course.' She looked up into his disbelieving eyes, and realised the jig was up. Oh, well, it had been fun while it lasted. 'What gave it away?'

'The carol singing,' he replied. 'No one who has ever heard me sing would even *think* of asking me to lead any carolling.'

Lena winced at the memory of music lessons at primary school. 'Good point.' She should have remembered that. 'But, you know, in years gone by you really *would* have been expected to do all those things.'

'Seriously?'

She nodded. 'Being Lord of the Manor isn't just lounging around while someone feeds you grapes, you know. It was a responsibility.' Even today, Toby and Autumn still held the Fire Festival up at Wishcliffe every autumn, and ran the Christmas celebrations at the house when December came. The church had taken over the Easter celebrations, and she'd never seen Toby or his brother or father in a rabbit costume, but the point still stood.

'Well, I'm not lord of anything,' Max said, uncomfortably. 'And I'm pretty sure no one around here ever wanted me to be. So that's the end of that.'

But it wasn't, Lena realised. It wasn't the end of anything.

Max had been an outcast in their village his whole life. And she'd spent forever trying to make Wells-on-Water the sort of place that didn't *have* outcasts. A place where everyone was welcome, and worthy of respect, kindness and support. A place where a person could ask for help—and get it. The sort of place where Max, if he were growing up there now, wouldn't have been bullied or looked down on or treated as less.

His return, even as an adult, gave her the chance to prove her efforts had been worthwhile.

'No, it's not,' she said, with dawning enlightenment. 'It's the start.'

'What do you mean?' There was genuine curiosity in his eyes as Lena searched for the right words to explain.

'You coming back here at all. I mean, Max, when you left, you weren't looking back, right?' It felt odd, talking to a man who was practically a stranger to her so openly. Except he *wasn't* a stranger.

For one night, sixteen years ago, she'd seen inside the soul of this man. Oh, not because they'd had sex, but because of the way they'd talked after, in a way they never had before or since.

It might have only been one night, a long time ago, but Lena had the strangest feeling that they were just picking up where they'd left off. That his soul hadn't changed at all.

Had hers? She didn't know.

'I never planned to return to Wells-on-Water at all,' he said, so flatly that she guessed he was now wondering again why he had.

'So the fact you're here now…it has to be the start of something new,' she said. 'You're not the boy you were when you left. You're the brother of the Viscount of Wishcliffe.'

'Half-brother,' he corrected. 'And I was always that.'

'*Acknowledged* half-brother, then. The point is, this is your chance to start again here. To be the person you want to be, not the boy people always assumed you were.'

He looked at her then, but she couldn't read his eyes. 'You assumed I was him, whoever he was, too. Didn't you?'

She met his gaze without flinching. 'Not that last night, I didn't.'

Hadn't he felt it, too, that final night? The connection between them? It was sixteen years gone, and it wasn't as if she'd wasted a *lot* of time thinking about it in the interim. But now he was back…Lena could feel it tugging at her again.

Max looked away. 'Perhaps.'

'You have a fresh start,' she pushed again. 'Not many people get that in the place where they grew up.'

'All because of who my father was?' He shook his head. 'If that's the only thing that gives me value and respect in this place, then I don't want it.'

'Then you'll have to give them something else to value, won't you?' Looking through the glass doors into the ballroom, Lena could see Kathy and Trevor watching her excitedly. They obviously thought she was fleecing their latest resident for donations.

And she could, she realised. She could do exactly that, and he'd probably let her. He might even be relieved to be able to hand over some money and be done with any guilt or obligations. To buy his way into the community and call it done. To never really find a place or a home here.

But she wouldn't. Because she had a feeling

that Max Blythe had a lot more to give to—and to gain from—Wells-on-Water. And if she had her way, she was going to make sure he did both.

She just needed to make sure she did it in a way that didn't involve giving up as much as she had last time they'd connected.

Or ever telling him how much that one night together had cost her.

Max wanted to ask Lena what she meant, about giving them something else to value, but before he could speak the doors crashed open and someone was tugging Lena's arm, demanding she come and deal with her brothers. So much for taking her away from *that* responsibility.

Max's memories of the Phillips brothers were far less fond than the ones he held of their sister, after all.

So he let her go, and enjoyed the solitude of the dark terrace a little longer, before venturing back inside and forcing himself to make polite conversation with people who had always disapproved of him.

Inside, the party continued. A band was playing at one end of the ballroom and people were even dancing—avoiding the spot where a waitress was on her hands and knees picking up what looked like a giant stack of squashed profiteroles.

But he couldn't stop Lena's words replaying in his head, even as he smiled politely and nodded at people who'd never given him the time of day before he had money and the right to use his father's name.

Give them something else to value.

Max had spent his childhood being shown through looks and whispers and pointed comments how little he mattered. How his mother's pretension—claiming her son, born out of wedlock, belonged to the most important man in the area—had only made him *less* important, not more. It was a strange existence—he'd somehow been both invisible and notorious at the same time. People hadn't liked to acknowledge him, not when he could see, but they'd talked about him endlessly behind his back.

Oh, at the local school the teachers had made an effort to treat him just like any other child sent to them for an education. Many of the staff drove in from surrounding towns and villages and probably genuinely hadn't cared whose son he was. But they couldn't influence what the parents told their kids, or the way those children had taunted or bullied him off the school grounds, especially once they'd moved up to the secondary school in Wishcliffe.

And the Phillips brothers had been the worst of the lot.

In fairness, it wasn't as if they'd *only* picked on him. Gary and Keith Phillips had been indiscriminate in their tormenting, he had to give them that.

And eventually he'd grown up enough to fight back. Which had just got him into another new world of trouble.

He looked up from a conversation with the vicar about the Sunday school to see if he could spot where Lena's brothers had got to. Just a hangover from the self-preservation tactics of his youth, he told himself, rather than a secret hope of seeing Lena again before she left. But there was no sign of any of them. Max suspected that Finn and Victoria would have had the Phillips brothers discreetly shown the door, so the party could continue more peaceably without them.

How much longer was it going to drag on for? And when could he reasonably make his excuses and head home? Even in London, parties like this really weren't his cup of tea. He preferred the intimacy of a private dinner, the chance to really talk around a subject and get down to what mattered. The surface chatter of these events grated on his nerves.

The vicar, clearly bored by Max's company, made his excuses and darted across the room to speak to someone else. *Anyone* else, Max suspected, and sighed.

It was just as well that no one really expected him to play Lord of the Manor here at Wells-on-Water. He was temperamentally unsuited for it.

'Those look like deep, dark thoughts,' Victoria said, appearing beside him, bump first. 'Penny for them?'

Max sighed again. Apparently it was becoming a habit. 'I was just thinking that it's probably for the best that the age of convivial lords of the manor who knew all their tenants by name and threw seasonal celebrations for them and so on is over. I don't think I'd be very good at it.'

Victoria laughed, high and bright, her eyes glinting in the candlelight. 'I think you're doing yourself down,' she said. 'But also, I think you'll find those times are not as dead and gone as you might think.'

He raised his eyebrows at that, and she continued to explain. 'Oh, I'm not saying you need to be the new best friend of everyone in Wells-on-Water. You're not running for Mayor—you don't need to win votes. But we're a *community* around here, Max. And the more you give to a community, the more you get out of it. You'll see.'

'Hopefully not,' he muttered, soft enough that she could pretend not to hear—even though her knowing smile suggested that she had.

She thought she knew better. That now he had the authority of his father's name, even if the man had never acknowledged him in life, Max would find a place here. A home. Acceptance in a place that had kept him on the outskirts his entire childhood. That had ostracised his mother while she'd lived, and forgotten her in death.

As if he would *want* that kind of community at all.

Except Lena's words were still echoing through his head. *Give them something else to value.*

He pushed them away. He wasn't here to prove his worth to these people. He didn't need to. He knew his value, and that was enough.

'Did Lena leave with her brothers?' He regretted asking as he saw Victoria's gaze turn fiercely curious.

'You and Lena got along well, then?' she asked. 'I saw you heading outside together...'

'We're old friends. We went to school together.' *We lost our virginities together.* He didn't admit, even to himself, that he'd been almost hoping they might be heading for a recreation of that night. Somewhere more comfortable than the back seat of a battered old car.

'Right.' Victoria looked disbelieving. 'Well, she's still here somewhere.' She scanned the room, then pointed across at the desserts table, where Lena was now helping the waitress clear up the last of the squashed-profiterole mess her brothers had presumably left behind. 'There she is.'

Which meant he had to cross the room towards her, because otherwise his asking after her sounded creepy—as if he just wanted to stalk her from a distance. And since he wasn't really sure *what* he wanted to do now he'd found Lena, he couldn't even make a reasonable excuse to Victoria.

'Oh, good,' Lena said as he reached her and the waitress, both kneeling on the floor. 'Can you grab some more cloths, please? From the kitchen.'

So Max found himself running to the kitchen for cloths, and then helping to clear up fresh cream and choux pastry from the ballroom floor, and only realising afterwards that he had chocolate-sauce stains on his shirt. And it was still better than making small talk with the vicar.

By the time they were done, the party was mercifully winding down. Lena dabbed ineffectually at the stains on his shirt, and he tried to pretend that her closeness wasn't doing things to his body that were inappropriate for a public gathering. 'You need to soak this, and fast,' she said.

Max batted away her hands to try and hold onto his composure. Besides, if she planned to touch him tonight, he wasn't going to waste it on cleaning his clothes. 'It's done for. If my dry-cleaner can't fix it, I'll buy a new one.' Maybe she'd help him take it off…

She tutted at that. 'So quick to throw away something that could still be of use to you. Come on.'

He wasn't entirely sure where she expected him to go, but he found himself following her all the same. 'I need to call a taxi. The guy who brought me gave me his card…' He patted his pockets looking for it. Usually he'd have driven; he liked to be in control of when he arrived and, more importantly, when he left a gathering like this. But he'd had a feeling that he'd need more than one drink to survive the occasion, and he never drove after more than one glass.

'Eddie brought you? Yeah, he's going to be in bed by now—he never works after nine these days.'

Max looked down at the card he'd finally located in his jacket pocket. *Eddie's Taxis.*

'Is there another taxi firm… No. Of course there isn't.' Because this was Wells-on-Water, not the city. Not even a town. He'd been away so long he'd forgotten the impossibility of rural village life. 'Guess I'll have to walk.' It was only a couple of miles. The fresh air would probably be good for him.

Lena rolled her eyes and grabbed his arm. 'Come on. I'll give you a lift. And then I can show you how to soak that stain properly.'

She said it so matter-of-factly, it took Max a minute to realise that Lena had casually invited herself into his home. At night. Maybe she'd expect a nightcap. Or maybe even more…

Was he imagining the heat between them tonight? He didn't think so. But then she concentrated so hard on the road as they made their way from Clifford House to the Manor House that he started to doubt himself.

And either way, he couldn't make assumptions.

'You really don't have to come in,' he said as they turned into the long driveway of the Manor House. 'Just giving me a lift is kind of you.'

'This village is good at kindness.' She shot him a sideways look. 'Well, usually.'

Kindness wasn't something Max really associated with the village. But he did associate it with Lena. Maybe this was just who she was, and he should say a polite goodnight and stop reading too much into it.

Her tiny, ancient yellow car juddered to a stop outside the Manor House, and she jumped out of the driver's seat before he could say anything at all and was already striding towards the front door. Max followed, still trying to persuade his body to stay calm and not get excited until Lena had told him exactly what she wanted. Maybe she just really had a thing about laundry…

Then she stopped, so suddenly he had to reach out and grab her arms to prevent himself from walking into the back of her. 'What is it?'

'You know we were talking about responsibility earlier?'

'Yeah?' What did that have to do with anything?

'Well, I think you just gained a new one.'

She stepped aside, but still it took him a long moment to see what she had obviously noticed the moment she approached.

The basket, sitting on the step outside his front door.

And even then, it wasn't until he heard the faint cry of a baby that he realised what she meant by 'responsibility'.

CHAPTER THREE

HOW DID SHE always end up in situations like this?

Okay, not *exactly* like this—Lena had never found a baby on the doorstep before—but situations where she couldn't do anything but help. It was past midnight, she was exhausted and wanted her bed, and yet here she was. Picking up a basket containing a squalling infant and carrying it over the threshold into the Manor House, while a shell-shocked Max Blythe followed behind.

She blamed her brothers, Lena decided. If not for their ridiculous antics at the party she wouldn't have been clearing up profiteroles and wouldn't have roped Max in to help. He wouldn't have got chocolate sauce on his shirt, and she wouldn't have been so irritated at his suggestion that he could just toss it away and buy a new one—had he never heard of the environment?—that she wouldn't have offered him a lift home, and she wouldn't have been there when he found the baby.

Although she knew that she wouldn't have left that party without saying goodnight to him. Without one last moment in his company, to see if she was imagining that the connection they'd forged sixteen years ago could still be hanging on by a thread, all this time later.

She knew herself well enough to know that the chances were she'd have been giving Max a lift home, anyway. Maybe even more…

Besides, it was just as well for the baby that she *was* there. Max's wide and terrified eyes in the sudden light of the hallway as he flipped the switch suggested he wasn't dealing so well with the new arrival.

Lena placed the basket on the parquet flooring, and reached in to pick up the baby, carefully supporting its head. It was small, young, but not newborn, as far as she could tell. Dressed as it was in a simple white sleep suit with tiny giraffes on, there was no hint as to whether it was a boy or a girl, but Lena was sure it would need changing soon enough and they could check.

But first…

'Something you want to tell me, Daddy?' she asked, raising her eyebrows at Max as she held the baby out to him.

Max recoiled, horror in his eyes. 'You think it's *mine*?'

'No, I expect someone just left it on your

doorstep because they thought you might be the parental sort. Of course it must be yours!' Why else would a mother abandon a baby here in the middle of the night, if not to reunite it with its father? 'I'd have thought you, of all people, would be more accepting of an unexpected child.' If his own mother had made different choices, this could have been him, couldn't it?

He flinched at that, but shook his head again. 'No, no. It can't be.'

His denial sounded more hopeful than as if he really believed it, Lena decided. But he still wouldn't take the baby.

'I should have known,' she muttered under her breath, feelings she'd buried sixteen long years ago starting to emerge once more.

'Known what?' he snapped back. 'That some crazy person would leave their baby here tonight?'

'That you wouldn't take any responsibility if they did! It's not like you called to check on me sixteen years ago, is it? For all you knew you could have come back to find a fully fledged teenager waiting for you.'

She hadn't meant to say it, but, Lena had to admit, seeing Max stagger backwards into the console table at the bottom of the stairs, horror clear on his face, it was kind of worth it. Actions had consequences, after all. She'd have thought *he'd* know that.

'I didn't...we used protection.'

'Because *that* always works.' The terror on his face hadn't dissipated. She almost didn't want it to. She wanted him to feel the same fear she had, back then, waiting for her period to come and knowing that if it didn't, her life as she knew it would be over. Protection or not, she'd been a teenage virgin who'd made a rash decision, and she'd known that if there *were* consequences, she'd be all on her own, with no way to contact him.

He was lucky it hadn't come to that. But a little terror wouldn't hurt him.

Eventually, too many years of making people feel better, of fixing situations, kicked in. 'Oh, relax. It was fine. But apparently you've never learned the lesson about follow-up. Assuming this little guy or gal is yours, I suggest you begin compiling a list of romantic partners who shared your bed around nine or ten months ago.'

The baby had fallen asleep in her arms, obviously soothed by the comfort of being held, and unbothered by their argument. Its tiny face was scrunched up inside the blanket, a small, knitted hat covering its head.

'I told you,' Max said, sounding desperate. 'It can't be mine.'

'Struggling to remember all the women's names, are you?' God, she'd actually thought he might be different. That night, sixteen years ago, she'd thought they'd had a connection—and he'd walked out without a backward glance. And then tonight, she'd honestly believed that his return to Wells-on-Water meant something. That he was ready to find his place in the community at last. Show them who he really was.

Apparently she'd misjudged him again.

'Quite the opposite.' Raking his hand through his hair, he moved closer, looking down at the baby in her arms with a softness she hadn't expected.

She tried to make sense of his words. 'What do you mean?'

'It's been a busy year.' He raised one shoulder in a half-shrug. 'I mean, first there was a big work contract, then Toby got in touch and since then… I guess it turns out that the baby really *can't* be mine. There hasn't been anyone in my bed in well over a year.'

Lena glanced down again at the bundle in her arms. Definitely *not* three months old.

'Well, you could have just said that.'

'Yeah. Sorry.'

For a long moment, they both just stared at the baby.

'So, what do we do now?' Lena asked.

Max huffed a laugh. 'You think I have any idea?'

The initial panic had faded from his face, but Lena could still see the fear in the shadows cast by the hallway lighting.

She couldn't leave Max on his own with the baby. From the look of him, he wouldn't know where to start with changing a nappy, let alone food and care for the tiny thing. Capable and successful businessman he might be. Family man he was not.

Not that she believed that she was the best option. She was the youngest of three siblings, and there hadn't been that many babies in her family after her. She'd done some childcare training, and first aid courses, partly to help with running kids' events at the hub, though. And she had friends with kids, and she'd at least absorbed some of the basics. If all else failed she knew how to do an Internet search for information.

More than that, she knew people who *did* know babies. And they owed her enough favours to get them through this.

'Should we call the police?' Max asked, suddenly looking up from the baby to meet her gaze. 'That's what you're supposed to do in situations like this, right?'

A chill skittered down Lena's back as she realised. If this baby wasn't Max's, and hadn't been left here by a desperate ex-girlfriend, then the mother had to be someone local. Which, since she knew everyone in Wells-on-Water, meant someone that Lena knew.

How desperate must she have been to leave the baby here?

She must have felt she had no other options. *If the community hub had still been running, she would have.* They'd had family-planning advice, confidential counsellors, when she could sweet-talk professionals into giving up their free time for the good of the village. If nothing else, the mother could have come to Lena, or Kathy, or whoever was manning the hub at the time, and they'd have been able to put her in touch with someone who could help.

The mother could even be someone she'd helped through the community hub before. Someone who needed support and kindness, not the police.

She knew how it felt to be that girl.

This was why her 'pet project', as Councillor Morgan patronisingly called it, really mattered.

This could have been her, sixteen years ago, if things had gone differently.

'Let's not get onto the police and everything yet,' she said, quickly. 'Let's see if we can sort this out ourselves, first.'

'Sort it out? How?'

Lena motioned to the basket. 'Have a look in there, for a start. See if there's a note, or supplies, or *something*.'

Watching him rifle through the blankets, Lena thought, fast.

She'd been teasing Max at the party about the responsibility of occupying the Manor House, but it hadn't all been a joke. Around here, people *did* still expect some loyalty from the lord of the manor, even if he didn't own the village any more. The Viscount of Wishcliffe had fulfilled the role for years, but the older hands would still remember when the first son and heir used to live at Wells-on-Water Manor House, and look after the tenants there. A first step to learning to care for a community.

Had someone left the baby here because they believed Max could provide and care for it better than they could? Because they were desperate, and didn't know what else to do?

Lena knew her community well. In times of crisis, they turned to each other, not the outside authorities. Maybe it wasn't the best way, but it was the only way the village knew.

If Max called the police, social services would get involved, and whoever left that baby on the doorstep could be in a lot of trouble, very fast.

But if they could find the mother themselves, maybe they could help.

'There are some nappies, and a bottle of formula,' Max said, just as the baby woke up and started squawking. 'And this note. But it doesn't make any sense.'

He held the paper out to her, and she scanned it, quickly.

This is your responsibility. I know you'll look after her for me.

Looked as if the mother believed Max was the father, even if he claimed it was impossible.

'Right,' Lena said, decisively. Time to take charge. 'In that case, we are going to feed and change the baby. And then I'm going to make some phone calls. Okay?'

Max nodded mutely. Sensible man.

Lena left him holding the baby. Literally. Despite the fact that he'd managed a full thirty-four years on the planet without ever holding one.

'I don't know what to do with it,' he'd protested, after they'd managed to change the baby's nappy—and discovered it was a girl in the process—and failed mightily at the feeding aspect of things.

'Just sit there and try not to scowl at her,' Lena replied, rolling her eyes at him. 'I'll try her again with the formula in a minute, but there's a call I want to make first.'

She disappeared off into the hallway again, leaving him in the front room, sitting on the uncomfortable leather sofa that had come with the house, wondering what the hell had happened to his night.

He looked down at the sleeping baby, suddenly very conscious that at least one person in the room was having a far worse night than him. Even if she didn't know it yet.

'How could someone just leave you there?' he whispered. 'I don't get it.'

Max shifted position slightly, trying not to jostle and wake the child in his arms. He'd always known that there were plenty of things about the world, about people in particular, that he didn't understand. But this one...he had a feeling this would always be beyond him.

'Who in their right mind would think that *my* doorstep was a good place to leave a baby? I mean, have they not *met* me?'

Maybe they hadn't, he realised. But they'd probably know about him. About his parentage. His past. His story.

Maybe *that* was why. Maybe they thought he'd understand.

But he didn't.

He tried to imagine what he'd have done, sixteen years ago, if Lena had tracked him down in London to tell him she was pregnant. Or if he'd returned here to find her with a sixteen-year-old daughter with her hair and his eyes. But he couldn't. The whole idea was so outside his sphere of experience, he just had no frame of reference.

One thing he knew for sure, it would have damned him for ever in the eyes of the village, for defiling their favourite daughter.

Maybe someone was targeting him because of his past. For his audacity in claiming his family name, his birthright, this house even. Except who would use an innocent baby to make a point like that? Just to drag his reputation through more mud? Even he didn't think the people of Wells-on-Water capable of that.

The thought crossed his mind that perhaps the baby could be connected to him in another way, since she obviously wasn't his daughter. Could she be Toby's? Except Max was one hundred per cent certain that Toby hadn't looked at another woman since he'd met Autumn, a year ago.

Could his father have had another illegitimate child? One who'd found themselves desperate and alone and turned to him for help?

But why wouldn't his father have acknowledged them in the same letter he'd left for Toby, where he finally accepted that Max was his child?

'It just doesn't make any sense,' he muttered.

'Are you talking to the baby, or to yourself?' Lena stood in the doorway, her arms folded across her chest, her eyes tired but amused.

'Both. I just… I don't understand.' He met her gaze with his own, feeling the fire coursing through him as he spoke. 'What if I hadn't been here, Lena? I'm not living here full-time, and I don't ever plan to. I'm still in London most weeks. I'm supposed to be heading back there in the morning…if I hadn't been here tonight, how long might that poor thing have been out there? What would have happened to it? How could someone *do* that?'

Sighing, Lena dropped into the armchair opposite him. Her pale blonde hair was coming loose from the pins holding it up at the back of her head, and strands of it framed her exhausted face. For a moment, she looked almost eighteen again. 'I don't know, Max. Sometimes people do really stupid things.'

Like sleep with a boy who'll never call to check on you afterwards, he thought, but didn't say.

This wasn't about them, or their history together. It wasn't about his own past, his mistakes—even if almost everything since he'd returned to Wells-on-Water seemed determined to remind him of it.

'I still say we should call the police,' he said, instead.

'And I'm not saying you're wrong.' Lena's words sounded heavy, weighing down the air between them. 'Just asking that we wait.'

'Why?'

'Because… Damn it, Max, you know this place as well as I do. Or you used to.'

'Yeah, I do. Seems to me like an abandoned baby of questionable parentage is prime gossip fodder around here. Isn't it best to get her out of the way before people start talking?' What kind of childhood could the poor thing have, abandoned before she could even sit up on her own, let alone fight her own corner?

'You're worried that people will talk about you?' She flashed him an irritated look. 'Newsflash, Max, they already are. I'm not sure they ever stopped.'

'I'm not worried about my reputation.' Well, he was. But not as much as other things. 'I'm trying to think about what's best for the baby.'

'Max…' Lena's expression faded from annoyance back to tiredness. 'I'm not saying they're not gossips but…the people of Wells-on-Water stick together.'

'As long as you're on the approved list,' Max muttered.

She ignored him and ploughed on. 'Whoever left the baby here has to be a local, I reckon. Someone who believed that the big house and the rich guy who lives there would look after their child while they couldn't.'

'Their first mistake.'

'And who would make sure the baby was cared for.'

'By calling the proper authorities,' Max finished, triumphantly.

'Max!' God, how long had it been since a woman had sounded so thoroughly infuriated with him? Probably not since his mother died.

'What?' The baby in his arms started to squirm, and he attempted to rock her in the hope of fending off a meltdown.

The first cry told him he'd failed. He was not a baby person, anyone could tell that—even this tiny scrap of a human that had been left on his doorstep.

He looked up at Lena to take the baby from him, but she just raised her eyebrows at him. 'I'd try her with the bottle again, if I were you.'

'Right. The bottle.' He reached for the small baby bottle that had been in the basket, along with a carton of formula milk. Lena had Googled temperatures, and they'd attempted some sort of sterilisation in the microwave, but the milk was cooling now. Was it still good? She'd rejected it the first time, when Lena had tried, but perhaps she was hungrier now.

Oh, I am really *not the right person to be doing this.*

As he tried to persuade the baby to take the teat between her lips and suckle, Lena began speaking again, softer this time, her frustration still evident but reined in.

'If we hand this baby straight to the authorities, that's it. It's done. There's no walking it back. But if we just give it a day or so to try and find the mother, see what the situation is there, and what we can do to help…'

Max sighed as it all started to make sense. 'You want to save them. Whoever left the baby. You want to save them.'

'I want to do the right thing,' Lena argued.

The words echoed in Max's head, as if they were doubled. As if he could hear his late mother saying the exact same thing, just as she had through his childhood.

Doing the right thing is more important than doing the easy *thing, Max Blythe.*

For his mother, the world had been black and white. There was the right thing and the easy thing. The easy thing—for both of them—would have been to lie about who his father was, to pretend. Especially when it had become clear that the old viscount was never going to acknowledge Max as his son. His mother could have made up a story about his parentage and people would have accepted it, even if the rumours still flew. And Max wouldn't have had to live with the public shame of a father who refused to admit he existed.

Maybe it wouldn't have made his childhood *easy*, exactly. But it would have been *easier*. And easier for the village to accept, too.

But it wasn't the *right* thing. And so his mother had vehemently stuck to her story in the face of all the arguments and the gossip. Max suspected that his father had even offered her money to make the rumours go away, but she hadn't taken that, either, however much easier *that* would have made their lives.

She'd done what was right, to her mind and her values, and damn the consequences.

Even today, Max wasn't sure if he admired her or hated her for it most.

He sighed. 'Who did you call, then?' he asked Lena, now.

'My friend, Janice. She's a GP. She's coming over now to check the baby over.'

'In the middle of the night?'

Lena shrugged. 'She's dedicated. And it's a baby, Max. Of course she's coming now.'

'Right.'

He half expected her to get up and leave, her work here done now she could hand over to the doctor. But instead, she leaned her head against the back of the armchair and let her eyes flutter closed.

'You're staying, then?' There was an unexpected bubble of hope in his chest at the idea. He didn't want to be alone with this—the baby, the responsibility, any of it.

And even if the evening hadn't gone at all the way he'd hoped…he didn't want Lena to leave. Not yet.

'Looks like it,' Lena said, without opening her eyes. 'For now, anyway.'

'That's…good.'

Maybe…maybe he just didn't want to be alone, at all. Which was a frightening proposition in itself.

In his arms, the tiny baby suckled another mouthful of milk, then pushed the teat away with her lips, her eyes closing too as she settled against him, apparently unaware that he was the least suitable person in the world for this job.

No, he definitely wasn't alone any more.

CHAPTER FOUR

LENA JERKED AWAKE, her neck aching from her awkward position in the chair, and her head fuzzy about what had woken her. Blinking, she sat forward, peering into the gloom of Max's sitting room. They'd left on only one small light, to try and help the baby sleep, and it seemed to have worked. On the sofa across from her, Max sat dozing, with the baby fast asleep in his arms.

It was almost…cute.

The baby was hidden from view mostly by blankets and the angle of Max's arm. But Max himself was perfectly visible—from the lock of dark hair that had fallen across his forehead, to the slight lines forming around his eyes. He looked younger in sleep, despite them—less weighed down by worry, or history, perhaps. And he looked far more comfortable holding the baby than he had when he was conscious.

In fact, if Lena had to find words to describe him right now, they would be 'adorably rumpled'.

Except she certainly wasn't supposed to be thinking of Max Blythe as adorably anything. And he'd probably glare lasers at her if she called him 'rumpled'.

Still. The point stood. And, in the dim light, Lena found she couldn't stop herself watching him sleep, the baby safe and secure in his embrace.

This really wasn't how she'd imagined this evening ending. And yet…

A knock at the front door reminded her that *something* had woken her—probably Janice arriving. Pushing herself up on the arms of the chair, she moved stiffly back into the hallway and pulled open the door.

On the doorstep, Janice looked her up and down, then gave a small smile. 'I have questions.'

'You're not the only one.' Lena stood aside to let her in, then shut the door behind her. 'The baby is sleeping, so if you want to ask them without a scream-along soundtrack, now is probably the time.'

'Okay. You said you found the baby on the doorstep?' Janice dropped her bag onto the floor then shrugged out of her coat.

Lena nodded. 'When we got back from the party at Clifford House there was a basket on the step. We looked inside and…baby.' Motioning with her left hand, she indicated the basket where it still sat on the hall table.

'No note or identifying details?' Janice poked around at the blankets in the basket.

'Nothing useful. Just a bottle, a carton of formula and a few nappies. And this note.' She handed it over.

Janice read it and grimaced. 'Max Blythe is the father, then?'

'Apparently not. According to him.' Lena believed him, but she could tell from Janice's expression that she wasn't convinced. Still, she let it pass, for now.

'And she seemed in good health?'

'I think so, but I'm no professional. That's why I called you.' Lena flashed her friend a grin. 'But she's had a little of the formula milk and we changed her nappy. She seems happy enough, considering.'

'Poor mite is too tiny to realise what's happening, I'd guess.' Janice tutted and shook her head.

'Any idea who the mother could be?' Lena asked. 'I mean, I know you can't tell me details, but you're GP to everyone in Wells-on-Water. If the mother is local she would have seen you for prenatal care…'

Janice looked thoughtful. 'Nobody springs to mind. But then…there's always the possibility that they didn't know—or didn't acknowledge—that they were pregnant at all.'

'And then panicked when the baby arrived,' Lena guessed.

'Exactly. Okay, next question—what were you doing here in the first place?'

'Are you asking that in your capacity as a doctor or my friend?'

'The latter,' Janice admitted, freely. 'I wasn't aware you were acquainted with Max Blythe. I mean, he's all anyone here has been talking about for weeks, and you never even let on that you knew him.'

That was the problem with having a best friend who'd only moved to Wells-on-Water for work, a few years before, when old Dr Mackay retired. As seamlessly as Janice had slotted into the tight-knit community, she didn't have the backstory of all the people there.

'I went to school with him; we're the same age,' Lena said. 'I guess I never mentioned it because everyone else around here already knew. Sorry.' She knew how Janice hated being reminded of her outsider status.

'So you were catching up on old times at the party, and came back here for a nightcap…?' Janice guessed.

'Not exactly.' Lena *really* didn't want to get into what sort of old times she and Max had to reminisce about, although she suspected Janice wouldn't let her get away with that for ever. 'He'd taken a taxi, and of course Eddie had already clocked off for the night by the time the party was over, so I offered Max a lift home. That was all.'

It was the complete truth. But Lena had to admit that a tiny part of her wondered what might have happened if there *hadn't* been a baby on the doorstep when they'd arrived. Would he have invited her in for a nightcap? Would they have started chatting more about old times? Would they have connected, the same way they had that last night before he left town—and would they have ended up sleeping together again?

If Janice had asked her yesterday, Lena would have said it was massively unlikely. Impossible even.

But here, at the Manor House, in the dark of the middle of the night, she wondered. And it didn't seem so completely impossible at all.

Still, she wasn't about to let on that, when she'd driven Max back to the Manor House, there had been…*possibilities*. Until they found the baby, anyway.

'Hmm. I'll believe you for now,' Janice said. 'But you better believe I'm going to have more questions later. *After* I've seen to my patient.'

'Of course you will.' Lena sighed. 'Come on, then. Let's wake up Sleeping Beauty.'

What mattered right now was the baby. *Not* whatever tonight's antics had stirred up inside her about the man she'd lost her virginity to, and the aftermath of that decision.

She'd deal with that later.

'Hmm? What? No. Don't send the giraffes in yet.' Max felt himself rising to consciousness, the concern about giraffes lingering from his dream into the waking world until he shook his head to rid himself of the last vestiges of sleep. There was a weight in his arms. Something he needed to do something about. To protect. Probably not a giraffe.

'Giraffes?' an amused voice asked. 'Deal with a lot of them in your business, do you?'

Max blinked his eyes open, and found Lena standing over him, one hand on his shoulder.

Lena Phillips. What is Lena Phillips doing in my house, talking about giraffes?

He frowned, glanced down, and the evening's craziness settled back into his brain when he saw the baby sleeping on his lap.

Right. A baby on his doorstep, and his first lover in his home.

And an unknown redhead watching them from the doorway, with a very curious expression.

'Janice—Dr Graham—is here,' Lena explained. 'So if you're done with the giraffes for now, I'll take the baby for her to examine.'

The redhead must be the doctor; that made sense. His brain was coming to life again now, and he knew he needed to gather his wits to figure all this out for the best, despite the lack of sleep and the strangeness of the day.

But the first thing—the most important thing—they all had to do was make sure the baby was okay.

He handed the sleeping bundle over to Lena, then followed anxiously as the baby gave a tiny squawk at being moved across the room towards Janice.

'Sorry about this, sweetheart,' the doctor murmured as she laid the baby on a clean blanket on the floor and set about unfastening her sleep suit.

'So, what were you dreaming about?' Lena sidled closer to him to ask. 'Apart from the giraffes, I mean.'

'I don't remember,' Max replied. 'It was just one those dreams, you know? Lots of things I was supposed to be doing, lots of people looking to me, and everything going wrong.'

'Like the giraffes.'

He sighed. 'Apparently so.' Giraffes were new in his dreamscape, but he wasn't fastening any particular meaning to them, all the same. At least, until he looked over to check on Janice and the baby and spotted the tiny cartoon giraffes on the sleep suit.

Clearly his subconscious was still working on this looking after a newborn thing.

'Does everything look all right?' he asked the doctor, who had her stethoscope out and was listening to the baby's heart.

'She's hale and hearty, as my grandmother would say.' Janice put away her equipment and began fastening the baby back into her sleep suit again. 'Just a week or so old, I think, but thriving as far as I can tell. I doubt she could have been out there waiting for you very long. In fact, I imagine the mother was lingering somewhere nearby to check that you found her okay.'

'What makes you think that?' Lena asked.

Janice shrugged. 'It's what I would do. Wouldn't you?'

'I suppose so,' Lena admitted.

Annoyance coursed through Max's tired body and he shot a glare at Lena, even though he knew it was as much his fault as hers. 'If we'd thought about it when we found her, we could have searched for the mother then and there and ended this thing in time for me to get a decent night's sleep.'

'You did the right thing,' Janice reassured

them. 'The most important thing was to make sure the baby was safe, and you did that. You called me.'

'The question is what we do now.' Max turned his attention back to the doctor. 'We should call the authorities, don't you agree?'

Janice and Lena exchanged a look he read all too clearly. *They don't think I understand. They think* I'm *the one being unreasonable here.*

And if the doctor was on Lena's side then he didn't stand a chance. His last hope for reason was gone.

'If we can't find the mother, we'll have to,' Janice admitted. 'I'm duty-bound as a doctor to do so.'

'But you can give us a day or so, right?' Lena pleaded. 'Just one day, to try and find her and sort all this out?'

'One day,' Janice conceded. 'And only because I know this village. The mother has to be one of us, right? And we look after our own.'

There it was again, that infuriating refrain. That holier-than-thou attitude of a village that had *never* looked after him—and now expected him to look after them. Heat rose inside him along with his temper, and Max bit down on the side of his cheek to keep it in check.

A cool hand on his arm calmed him, and he looked over to see Lena watching him under worried brows. 'It's just one day,' she said softly. 'Just to be sure. I know you don't owe anyone here anything, but…she could be scared, Max. She could be desperate and scared and need our help.'

His anger and frustration ebbed away at her touch, her gentle words, and Max couldn't help but remember another day, many years ago, when she'd done the same—stopping him from punching one of her brothers, the younger one, he thought. That was after he'd grown into his height, and his strength. Her brothers had never bothered him again after that day, though.

Strange how, for someone he'd never have claimed to know well, Lena had been there at so many important moments in his life. And here she was now, with this.

The curse of the small village, he supposed. That was all. *Someone* had to be there, after all, and there weren't that many people in Wells-on-Water of his age. It was nothing more than that.

He pulled his arm away from her hand. 'Fine. We'll look after her tonight, and try to find her mother in the morning. But after that we're calling the police.'

Lena's smile warmed him again, but in a very different way.

'In that case, you'd better come up with a name for her,' Janice said as she packed away her things. 'Even if she's only here for twenty-four hours, you can't keep calling her "the baby" the whole time.'

Max and Lena exchanged a look.

'I remember bringing a squirrel home once, and my mother wouldn't let me name it because then I'd think I could keep it,' he said. Was it totally crazy to worry the same thing about Lena in this situation? Not himself, though. Probably.

'Well, we're definitely not keeping her,' Lena said. 'But Janice is right. We can't keep calling her The Baby.'

Max stared at the tiny, scrunched-up, dozing face of the baby as she lay in Janice's arms. 'Willow. For the trees that grow down by the river, on the edge of the village.' It was only after he said it that he remembered that was the same spot he'd last seen Lena before leaving Wells-on-Water, after taking her back to the party.

Janice nodded. 'Good name.' She handed the baby back to him, and Max took her, almost without thinking, then panicked, juggling her slightly to try and hold her correctly.

'Willow it is, then,' Lena said, and smiled at him.

Janice left them with a bag full of newborn nappies, a microwave steriliser, formula and more bottles, along with baby wipes, changes of clothing, muslin cloths and other things Lena hadn't even had a chance to sort through yet. She'd never realised that a baby required quite so much *stuff*.

Their first priority, however, was sleep—for them, as well as Willow. 'We'll never be able to function tomorrow if we don't get *some* rest,' Max pointed out, perfectly logically.

Without a cot for Willow, they decided she'd have to sleep in the Moses basket she'd arrived in. Together, they shifted all the supplies—and the baby—upstairs, where Lena stopped on the landing and stared at the bedroom doors before her.

'You want me to stay the night?' She was almost certain he did, given his earlier words, but she'd never really envisioned actually sleeping in a bed in his home. Other things, perhaps. But not sleeping.

And *whose* bed?

'If you don't object,' Max replied. 'I figure we can take shifts, right? You get some sleep first—since I had a nap downstairs—then we'll swap after a few hours.'

'And you'll look after the baby while I sleep?'

'Of course.' Max frowned, suddenly looking uncertain. 'Well, once you show me what I need to do.'

Lena pulled a face. 'What makes you think I know?'

'Didn't Janice tell you?'

'No more than she told you.' In all honesty, she *did* have a pretty good idea, but it would do Max good to have to figure things out, too, rather than just assuming the woman would know all there was about childcare.

'Oh.' Max gave her a tired smile. 'Back to Google, then, huh?'

Between them, they got Willow changed and fed again—after finding instructions for the steriliser online. While Max fed her—modifying his curse words to ones suitable for tender ears after her first glare—Lena read up on sleep for newborns in the book she found at the bottom of Janice's bag of tricks.

'It says here she'll probably only sleep for a few hours at a time at her age.'

'A few hours sounds positively blissful right now,' Max admitted, dribbling milk from the bottle all over Willow's clean sleep suit, then hurriedly getting the teat back between her lips at the first cry. 'What time is it, anyway?'

Lena checked the clock on her phone and winced. 'Just gone three-thirty in the morning. Urgh, I'm too old to stay up this late.'

Max chuckled at that. 'You're only thirty-four, the same as me.'

'Yeah, well, I feel older at three in the morning.' She yawned, her jaw cracking at the movement.

'Go to bed,' Max said. 'Really. I've got this now. Probably. Top of the stairs, second door on the left. It's the guest room.'

Oh, but that sounded tempting. 'What about you?'

He still looked uncertain, but the determined set of his jaw told Lena that Max wasn't going to let something as tiny as a baby break him.

'I told you. We'll take shifts. The basket is in my room so, once we're done here, I'll take her up and see if I can get her to sleep in it. If I can't, I'll sit up with her a while longer. Then I'll sleep once you take over.' That, she had to admit, sounded like the most likely outcome.

'Should I set an alarm on my phone?' Lena was already edging towards the door, the lure of a soft mattress and a warm duvet too much to resist.

Willow gave a sharp cry as the bottle slipped from between her lips again. Max gave Lena a tired smile. 'I don't think we'll really need it. Do you?'

Lena awoke some time later, cocooned in blankets in Max's spare room. It felt as if she'd only been asleep for moments, but the sunlight streaming through the open curtains said otherwise. Groping for her phone, her eyes barely open, she checked the time. Almost seven. It had to be her turn to take over with Willow by now.

A wail from somewhere nearby confirmed her conclusions. Stumbling out of the bed, she pulled her dress from the night before back over her head, then made her way towards the sound, pinning it down to the room next door. She contemplated knocking, but if Max was sleeping through Willow's cries a simple knock wouldn't wake him, and if he was already awake he probably wouldn't hear it over them.

She pushed the door open and peered inside. Max had obviously had the energy and foresight to actually close his curtains before bed, so the room was still dark. But she could hear the low rumble of Max's voice, and just make out his figure where he leaned over the Moses basket. As she watched, he picked the baby up and held her close to his chest, his shoulders slumped with obvious exhaustion. But the long night seemed to have at least made him more comfortable with the idea of holding the baby.

'Come on, Willow, just another half an hour, yeah? You've had your milk, your nappy is dry, I'm running out of ideas here, sweetheart. I mean, trust me, you don't want me to sing to you. Half an hour and we'll wake Lena up and see if she has any ideas.'

'I don't know about ideas, but I do have the energy that comes from three hours passed out in your spare room,' she said.

Max turned at the sound of her voice. 'Three hours doesn't really seem like enough.'

'Looks like three more than you got,' she pointed out.

He shrugged, but the movement seemed to exhaust him even more. 'I napped a bit here and there. Mostly by accident.'

Holding out her arms, Lena waited for him to place the baby in them. She'd stopped crying, at least. She seemed happier when she was being held. Lena supposed she could understand that.

'You're sure?' Max asked.

Lena rolled her eyes. 'You don't think I can cope?'

'I don't think *I* could. Or maybe that should be can.' With a tired smile, he settled Willow into her arms. 'Her milk and bottles are in the kitchen; steriliser is by the microwave. But she just had a bottle twenty minutes ago—well, some of it, anyway, most of it seemed to end up down me. And I've changed her nappy again—although you might want to check that, because I'm not sure I got it right—'

'Max. We'll be fine. Get some sleep.' Lena

couldn't help but be a little amused at the way he'd flipped from wanting to make Willow someone else's problem to total concern for the tiny baby. They must have bonded overnight, she supposed.

'Yeah, okay. G'night.' He was collapsed on the bed, eyes closed, before she and Willow even left the room.

'Good morning,' she whispered to the baby as snores began to echo through Max's bedroom door.

Her head still spun a little from tiredness, so she took the stairs carefully, slowly making her way down to the kitchen. Once there, of course, she realised that without the basket she had nowhere to put the baby down while she made coffee, which was definitely going to be a problem sooner or later. She didn't want to risk scalding the poor mite, but she also couldn't exactly put her down on the cold stone floor of the kitchen.

Willow started to fuss again as she stared longingly at the kettle, so Lena moved away from temptation and stepped into the hall. She'd barely had a chance to explore the ground floor of the Manor House the night before, and now seemed like the perfect opportunity. If she was lucky, she might even find a nice, thick blanket to use as a play mat or something.

As she paced around the rooms of the Manor

House, however, the only thing Lena found was the reason why Max had shepherded her into the small, front sitting room he used as a study the night before: it was the only reception room with any furniture in it at all.

'He's been here on and off for weeks, Willow,' she murmured as she walked, gently jostling and rocking the baby, since that seemed to make her happiest. 'Why hasn't he bought any furniture yet? It's not as if he can't afford it.'

That was one point that the local rumour mill was all agreed on, when it came to Max Blythe. Whatever he'd been doing away from Wells-on-Water for the last sixteen years, it had made him a very rich man.

The answer came to her as she wandered back towards the kitchen, Willow content in her arms.

'He doesn't think he belongs here. Even now.'

Lena knew that Max's childhood hadn't been all fun and games in the village. They might not have been friends, exactly, but in a place as small as Wells-on-Water she'd had a front-row seat to the way people treated him by default.

She'd told him the night before that coming back gave him a chance to prove them all wrong. Maybe helping with Willow was the first step to that. To finding his place here.

But they only had one day to make it count.

Just twenty-four hours—less now she'd wasted some of it sleeping—to find Willow's mum *and* Max's place in the village.

'I'd better get to work, then, I suppose,' she whispered. Willow gurgled in agreement.

Taking a seat at the kitchen table, Lena stared at her phone and wondered how long she had before Max woke up. Long enough, she decided.

This was just like any other community project she'd taken on over the years, really. And if there was one thing Lena Phillips was *brilliant* at, it was bringing this community together.

And she knew just where to start.

CHAPTER FIVE

MAX CAME UP from sleep slowly, as if he were pushing his way through a vat of his mum's treacle pudding, sponge and syrup filling his ears. But even that sensation couldn't completely muffle the noises coming from downstairs.

Voices.

Laughter.

The scrape of furniture moving.

Since he had very little furniture here at the Manor House, that last was particularly worrying.

He blinked, and the night before came back to him, causing him to sit up so fast his head spun. Lena. The basket. *Willow.*

The Moses basket beside the bed sat empty, but since he vaguely remembered Lena coming and taking the baby before he passed out that wasn't too surprising. He was more concerned about whatever else Lena had seen fit to do with his home while he was asleep.

He washed quickly in the en-suite bathroom, running wet hands through his hair to try and tame it, and switched his clothes for cleaner non-black-tie ones. Then, he jogged down the main staircase—and stopped just before the turn in the stairs to stare down over the bannister at his hallway.

It was packed. As far as he could tell, half the village was in his home, and it looked as if they'd brought the contents of their own houses with them. He recognised a few faces from the party the night before—rather less dressed up than they had been then, of course. Others he picked out as familiar from his childhood. Older now, but still the same in his memories.

He turned away from those ones.

In the middle of it all stood Lena—still dressed in the sparkly, shimmery pale blue dress she'd worn for last night's party, although given the way it pooled around her feet he suspected she'd foregone the heels. Beside her, Janice held Willow, cooing down at the baby, while Lena directed villagers left and right into his main drawing room, or the kitchen, depending on what they were carrying.

And all the time they were talking. Every one of them chattered and gossiped away without ceasing. About the baby, the secret mother, the house…him.

He couldn't stand it any longer.

Treading heavily, he swung himself around the bannister to stand at the top of the final set of stairs, looming over the gathering in the hallway. It only took a moment for the house to fall silent.

From the centre, Lena smiled up at him, her eyes wide and guileless. 'Max! You're up. Great.'

At the sound of her voice, the tension in the hall dissipated. Conversations started up again, and people began moving around once more, shifting baby supplies and other such things from one room to another.

Robbed of a dramatic moment—or the chance to throw everyone out of his damn house—Max sighed and made his way down the rest of the stairs to where Lena was waiting for him.

'What, exactly, is going on here?' he asked, his voice tight. 'Why are all these people in my house?'

Lena's smile dimmed a little with uncertainty. 'Well, I was thinking that if we only have twenty-four hours to find Willow's mum, we need to get moving, and we need some help. So I started calling around to see if anyone had any intel, or theories about who the mother might be. And then…' She trailed off, looking around her helplessly at the frenzied activity of the locals.

'And then?' Max pressed. 'Because I really

don't see how information gathering led to whatever the hell this is.' How long had he been asleep, anyway? It couldn't have been more than a few hours.

How in the world had Lena managed all this in such a short space of time?

'I had to tell them what was going on, of course, to get their help,' Lena said slowly. 'And, well, when people heard that you were taking care of Willow—'

'*We're* taking care of Willow,' he corrected her. There was no damn way he was doing this alone.

'They wanted to help,' Lena finished.

'Help. How is invading my house and gossiping about me helping?'

'They didn't *invade*.' Exasperation leaked out of Lena's voice. 'They brought supplies—more nappies and formula, baby clothes, a bouncy chair for Willow, a proper play mat, that sort of thing.'

'Where do you want the coffee machine, Lena?' A guy Max didn't recognise walked past with a large box in his arms, shouting the question as he moved.

'Um, kitchen, please. It's that way—I think Kathy is setting things up in there,' Lena replied, pointing.

'And has Willow developed a sudden urge

for caffeine since I fell asleep three hours ago?' Max folded his arms over his chest and raised his eyebrow in a way that past employees had told him was particularly intimidating.

Lena just rolled her eyes. 'The coffee is for us, idiot. So are the meals Trevor is stocking the freezer with, and the spare furniture Janice's husband Tom is setting up in the drawing room, so Willow has a play space you won't mind getting covered in milk and baby sick.'

'They brought actual furniture?' Max was well aware that the furnishings of the Manor House were somewhat lacking. Beyond his bedroom, the spare bed, and the sitting room that also served as his study, he hadn't really thought about it. But after only a few hours in his home, most of them delirious with sleep deprivation, it seemed that Lena had.

Lena shrugged. 'Just spare stuff. You know, a sofa that was cluttering up someone's garage, someone else's old rocking chair—that'll be good for feeding her, or napping with her, come to that.'

'Seems like an awful lot of stuff for twenty-four hours' worth of babysitting,' Max pointed out.

She flashed him a smile that looked like trouble. 'Well, I guess we'll see how it goes, won't we?'

Before he could question her further on that,

someone else was dragging her away to look at something, and he realised that Willow was crying in Janice's arms. Probably she hated this circus as much as he did.

He wanted to leave this whole mess to everyone else, to all the people who had taken over his home at a word from Lena. But he was *responsible* for the baby. That was what the note had said. And until he passed that responsibility on to someone else…well. He planned to live up to it.

He didn't believe in always doing the Right Thing with the sort of zeal his mother had, or even the way Lena seemed to—not least because he wasn't convinced there always was one right thing to do. But he sure as hell wasn't going to treat an innocent baby the way the haters in the village had treated him his whole life—as an outcast, a disgrace, just because of who her parents were or what they'd done.

They were helping now, but Max knew better than to believe that would last past this initial flurry of do-gooder-ness. If they didn't find Willow's mother, she'd always be the abandoned child, the one nobody wanted.

Max wanted better than that for her.

But for now, the least he could do was take her away from this circus.

'I'll take her,' he told the doctor. Janice beamed

as she handed over the child. 'She probably needs a change and another bottle.'

He hoped so, anyway, since that was basically all he knew how to do with her. That and cuddle her to sleep. All of them imperfectly.

He'd leave Lena to the chaos out here and look after the baby. Something he'd never imagined he'd find himself doing out here in Wells-on-Water.

And then he was going to do something else he'd never imagined doing.

He was going to call his brother.

It took a while to clear out all her helpers once things were set up. Lena suspected that was because they'd all always wanted a glimpse inside the Manor House and this was the best opportunity they were likely to get.

Still, eventually it was clear that there was nothing left to do, and nothing left to be gained by lingering since Max had sequestered himself with Willow in his study. And so, slowly, the locals began to depart—still gossiping as they went.

Lena could understand why Max might feel uncomfortable amongst all the curious chatter. She knew how much of his childhood had been filled with people talking about him—about who his father really was, about his mother's words and actions, even about the trouble he'd himself got into and whether it was inevitable, given his background.

She'd been gossiped about enough herself through her life, too, even if it was more affectionately than Max had been subject to. She was a familiar and popular face around the village from her youth, given that her father ran the local pub. And she was a figure of pity or at least sympathy after her mother died.

The only girl in a family of men after that, she'd been sort of adopted by the older women of the village—all of whom seemed to have an opinion on what she wore, who she kissed, who she dated and what she did with her life. She'd be forever thankful that no one had seen her and Max together that last night, sixteen years ago, because if they had they'd still be gossiping about it now, she was sure.

Probably even more, now, given that she'd spent last night in Max's home.

She let out a sigh as the door swung behind the last visitor—or almost last, she realised, as Janice appeared from the drawing room they'd turned into a baby room.

'I brought you some clothes to change into, if you want to get out of that dress,' her friend said, holding out a bag.

Lena took it gratefully. 'Thanks. As much as

I love this dress, it's hardly suitable for babysitting.'

Janice leant against the doorframe and looked her up and down. 'Could be perfect for seducing our new lord of the manor, though.'

'Do you really think that's what I'm doing here?' Lena asked incredulously.

'Nah. You're far too nice for that. But you could be,' Janice said. 'I mean, you have to have noticed the way he looks at you.'

'Mostly with annoyance,' Lena replied.

Shaking her head, Janice moved to perch on the stairs. 'I don't know the man, but annoyance was when he found his home full of people. When he showed up on the stairs I thought he was going to yell and toss us all out on our ears.'

'So did I,' Lena admitted.

'But then you whispered to him and he turned into a softie. He even volunteered to go change Willow's nappy and give her a bottle.'

'That was just because he wanted to escape being here,' Lena said. But she had to admit—to herself, if not to Janice—that she was surprised at how easily Max had taken to looking after the baby. She didn't get the impression that Max had much experience of looking after things—or being looked after, for that matter.

'So, did all this activity achieve anything more than access to the Morrisons' old coffee machine and other essential supplies?' Janice asked. 'Did you get any leads on Willow's mother?'

Because that was what it had all been about, really—even if Lena had to remind herself of that from time to time. 'Not much.' She hiked her dress above her knees and sat down beside Janice on the stairs. 'Oh, people had plenty to say, but you know what they're like. Not much of it had to be grounded in reality.'

'And they were all more excited about getting to poke around the Manor House and coo over the baby, anyway,' Janice guessed.

'Pretty much. What about you? Anything in your patient files that might give us a clue?'

Janice shook her head. 'Not really. I have a few people I want to follow up on at home, just in case. But only one of the pregnant women I've seen lately was due around now, and she was here today helping and still very pregnant.'

'Esther Jones,' Lena guessed. 'Right.'

'You really didn't hear anything from anybody?'

Lena leant back, her elbows resting on the stair above them. 'Plenty of theories but no evidence. Mrs Jenkins from the shop is adamant that it has to be the Havers's daughter, because she's been in buying ready salted crisps and Diet

Coke, and that was all Mrs Jenkins's daughter could stomach when she was pregnant.'

'Never mind that Milly Havers was parading down the high street in what Hillary Jenkins deemed an "unacceptably cropped top" last weekend,' Janice said.

'She seemed to have forgotten that, yes.' Lena sighed. 'I don't know. I've got Terri Jacobs subtly raising it at the secondary school in Wishcliffe, since that's where most of our teenagers go, and Fiona is going to activate the parent phone tree, in case the mother *is* a scared teen who managed to hide her pregnancy. Dominic is going to speak about it in his sermon on Sunday—and he promises it will be all forgiveness and support and asking for help, not judgement. And I spoke off the record to Heather at the hospital, to see if she can find out anything. But I can't imagine I'm going to get many answers inside Max's twenty-four-hour deadline.'

'Then you'll have to convince him to extend it.' Janice got to her feet, brushing down her jeans as she stood. 'At least until we've had a chance to gather more answers.'

'And how, exactly, am I supposed to do that?'

Turning, Janice raised her eyebrows and flashed Lena a naughty smile. 'I'm sure you'll think of something.' Whatever reaction she saw in Lena's face made her laugh. 'Oh, I'm kidding. Like you'll have the chance with the baby here and everything. But I still reckon he wants you. Actually, you could probably seduce him without very much effort at all during one of Willow's naps…'

Lena bit her bottom lip, then said, 'What if I told you I already had?'

Janice's eyes flew open wide. 'What? When? Last night?'

'No, no. Years ago. Before he left Wells-on-Water after we finished school.'

'Wait, he was the guy you lost it to in the back of a car? The boy you shared a soulmate-like moment with?' Oh, Lena was regretting telling her that after too many glasses of wine one night. 'Why did you never tell me that?'

'Because he was gone. Because we were eighteen and stupid. Because it didn't really matter.' Except it had. It had mattered to her. Not just because it was her first time—although she'd tried to convince herself ever since that that was all it was.

But now he was here, and she was stuck playing house with him until they found Willow's mother, she had to admit the truth.

'Didn't matter?' Janice asked, eyebrows arched. 'And how is that argument holding up in the face of fully grown Max Blythe?'

'Badly,' Lena admitted. 'I don't know. He's

not the boy I shared that night with. But I have to admit…I'm kind of intrigued by the man he's become.'

Janice glanced towards the closed study door. 'I can't say I blame you. So, go get yourself freshened up and changed, then go see if you can't reconnect enough to convince him to give you the time to find Willow's mum.'

Max felt far more relaxed with the study door shut on the mayhem outside, even if he wasn't actually alone. Willow lay peacefully in his arms and he wished he'd had the foresight to snag that bouncy chair Lena had mentioned so he could actually put her down.

As it was, he made do with the travel change mat and bag Janice had hung on his shoulder to lay her comfortably on the floor to replace her nappy—slightly more securely this time. Then, after using the anti-bac wipes on his hands, he settled onto the sofa to feed her while he rehearsed what he wanted to say to Toby in his head.

He waited until Willow had finished her bottle and was dozing, milk drunk, on his lap before actually reaching for the phone—cautiously, without sudden movements, in the hope that the baby might actually stay content long enough for him to have a conversation.

'Hello? Max?' Toby's voice sounded faintly panicked on the other end of the line. 'Is everything okay? What's happened?'

'Everything's fine,' Max replied, even though it wasn't strictly accurate. 'Why wouldn't it be?'

'Um, because you're calling me?' Toby said. 'That's not exactly an everyday occurrence. Or an ever occurrence.'

'I've called you before.' Surely he had to have phoned his half-brother at least once or twice since Toby got in touch. Hadn't he?

'You've *emailed* me before,' Toby corrected him. 'Even texted me, once. But call? Never.'

'Well, I'm calling now,' Max said grumpily. 'Because I need your...advice, I guess.'

'You are absolutely certain that the world isn't ending?' Toby joked.

'Mostly.' Although, given that he was sitting in his study with a baby in his lap and half of Wells-on-Water in his hallway, there was room for doubt.

'Sounds ominous. What's going on?'

It took surprisingly little time to recap the events of the previous twelve hours—returning to the Manor House with Lena to find Willow on the doorstep, and the subsequent home invasion by the locals. Toby didn't interrupt, although Max was sure he heard him smother a laugh when he got to the part about hiding in his study.

'Okay, so I have many questions,' Toby said, when he was finished. 'But my first one has to be: Why was Lena Phillips coming home with you at midnight?'

Max let his head fall back to stare at the ceiling. *Of course* that was what Toby would choose to focus on. He was all loved up with his new bride and a baby on the way, so he was seeing romance everywhere.

'She gave me a lift home from Finn and Victoria's party,' he said shortly. No way he planned to mention his and Lena's history together—or that he'd kind of been hoping that history might repeat itself, until Willow had appeared.

'Right,' Toby said disbelievingly. 'You know, I've always liked Lena...'

'Well, that's great for you. But since she's currently reconfiguring my entire house for a baby who doesn't belong to me, do you think we could maybe concentrate on what actually matters here?'

He hadn't meant to raise his voice, but the little cry Willow gave suggested that he had anyway.

'Is the baby there with you right now?' Toby asked, sounding amused.

'She didn't like all the chaos outside, either,' Max grumbled. 'And it was time for her bottle.'

Toby was unexpectedly silent at that revelation.

'So, are you going to tell me what to do?' Normally, Max hated being ordered around, in any circumstance. And Toby was technically his *little* brother, which made asking even worse. But he was so far out of his depth, and so damn tired, he'd take what he could get.

'Like you'd listen to me anyway,' Toby said, with a laugh. 'But honestly, Max, I don't see that you have very many options. You're right that you need to alert the proper authorities *and* Lena's right that the villages around here look after their own.'

'I told her I'd give her twenty-four hours to find the mother.'

'Do you think that'll be enough?'

'No.' He'd known it when he said it, and he suspected Lena had, too. 'So what's my next move?' he asked, after a long moment's silence.

'I'm thinking,' Toby replied. 'Okay, so the note you found with the baby—'

'Willow.'

'Right, Willow. The note hinted that she was your child?'

'Yes. Except she *can't* be.' And Max was just loving having to explain his lack of sex life to multiple people over the last twenty-four hours.

'But what if you thought there was a chance that she was?'

Max blinked. Either he was particularly slow this morning or Toby wasn't making any sense at all. 'What do you mean?'

'I mean, if Willow *was* your child, then you wouldn't have to hand her over to the authorities, right? You'd get to keep looking after her until Lena found the real parents.'

'So you're suggesting we contact the authorities…but claim she's *mine*?' That sounded even more crazy than anything his sleep-deprived mind had come up with.

'Just a thought,' Toby said. 'I mean, to be honest, you don't sound like you're all that keen to hand her over to social services.'

Of course he was. That was exactly what he wanted to do—hand her over to the proper authorities and get his life back to normal. Why wouldn't he?

'I'm sure Lena would stay on a little longer to help out, too,' Toby added slyly.

'She'd better.' Not that he was thinking too hard about why he wanted Lena to stick around. Not while he was holding an innocent child.

'Plus it sounds like all the locals are pitching in. You won't be short of babysitters, if I know the people of Wells-on-Water.'

Something else that was confusing the hell out of him. Because Max *did* know the locals, and this was not the sort of behaviour *he* expected from them at all. 'I just don't understand why everyone is here, helping.'

'That's what people do in times of need or crisis, isn't it?' Said with all the confidence of a man who had never been on the receiving end of that sort of kindness, because he'd never *had* that kind of need. Toby was the legitimate son, after all.

Not like Max.

'Not in my experience.' He knew the words sounded bitter, and, from the sudden silence on the other end of the line, he expected that Toby knew what he was referring to, as well.

The brothers had talked very little about their shared father, and the past hurt and betrayal between them. It had always seemed more important to focus on the future they could build together, instead. But now Max wondered if they'd ever really be free to be family, to be brothers, if they *didn't* address the elephant in the room.

The fact that their father's refusal to admit that Max was his son had made Max's childhood hellish.

'How do you mean?' Toby said, after a moment. Max wondered if he'd come to the same conclusion as he had and was facing it head-on.

But right now wasn't the time to get into the details, the bitter reminiscing. He had Willow to worry about, in the here and now, and that was more important than anything that had happened in the past.

He really hadn't expected the visceral connection he felt to the tiny child, especially since he *knew* she couldn't be his. But he had to admit, it was hard to imagine just handing her over to social services in—he checked his desk clock—fifteen hours.

'I just mean that, growing up here in the village, I remember people taking more of a judgemental line than a supportive one.' If people out there were slating Willow's mother for her actions, he hadn't heard it. Everything he'd overheard had been about helping the baby, and finding the mother to make sure *she* was all right.

He hadn't expected that. And he wasn't convinced it would last.

'Maybe they've all learned something, over the years,' Toby said mildly. 'If I were you, I'd ask Lena about that.'

'Lena?' he repeated in confusion. 'Why Lena?'

Toby chuckled. 'Because I think that for every community event, every campaign—from the hunt for Jayden's missing rabbit to the Teddy Bears' Picnic treasure hunt and party to raise money for the local community hub—Lena has been at the heart of it. Wells-on-Water *has* changed since you grew up there, Max. And a lot of that has to do with Lena.'

It shouldn't surprise him. In a way, it didn't. Even at school, she'd always been on the organising committee for school proms and fetes, or the one single-handedly running a campaign for recycling bins in the canteen.

Unbidden, a memory floated into his head. That last night before he'd left, he'd asked if she would go, too. Not with him, exactly, but at all. Even then he'd thought that a backwater village like Wells-on-Water was too small, too petty minded, for someone who shone as brightly as Lena Phillips.

'Maybe,' she'd said. *'But I think I'd always come back. I belong here. And there's too much that needs doing.'*

'Couldn't you do it somewhere else?' he'd asked.

'Why would I?' She'd turned then, he remembered, her golden hair spread out over his bare arm as she'd looked up at him with glittering eyes. *'Why try to fix the world without starting here in my own backyard?'*

'Of course it does,' he murmured.

Another reason to try to hold onto Willow a little longer so they could search for her mother floated into Max's mind. He'd run out on Lena sixteen years ago, and never even called her after to check in. She'd been right to call him out on that.

But maybe he could prove to her that he wasn't the immature boy he'd been then any longer, by sticking around and pitching in this time. By helping Willow, and hopefully her family, too.

Outside in the hallway, he heard the front door slam shut, and a single set of footsteps retreating upstairs. Craning to listen, he realised that the constant noise that had woken him that morning had faded.

'I think they've gone,' he told Toby, who laughed.

'Then it's safe for you to come out of hiding. And I'd better go, anyway. I think Mrs Heath has lunch ready for us, and Autumn really doesn't like waiting for food these days.'

Since Autumn was nearly nine months pregnant, Max wasn't surprised. 'Okay. Enjoy your lunch. And…thanks, Toby.'

'Any time,' his brother said easily, before he hung up.

And strangest of all, Max really believed he meant it.

CHAPTER SIX

LENA TOOK ADVANTAGE of the small en-suite bathroom attached to the room Max had shown her to the night before to shower quickly, before changing into jeans and a T-shirt. Janice hadn't packed much beyond the clothes, though, so she had to make do with the shower gel and deodorant she found in the bathroom, alongside the guest towels, which she guessed were spares Max had lying around, as they resulted in her smelling just like him.

Which wasn't distracting at all.

Still, she felt a dozen times better for being clean, and out of last night's underwear and party clothes. She bounced down the stairs to find Max, but the study he'd retreated to was empty.

Pausing, she sniffed the air.

Coffee.

Lena smiled, and headed for the kitchen, where she found Willow settled into the bouncy chair someone had brought, her eyes wide as she took in her surroundings. Or not. Lena had a feeling that babies couldn't see very far at all. But whatever Willow was looking at, she seemed content with it.

'You figured out the coffee maker, then?' Lena leaned against the kitchen table as Max handed her a steaming cup with frothy milk.

'It wasn't exactly rocket science. Not like this thing.' He motioned towards another machine on the counter. 'I think it's supposed to make her milk, or heat it, or something, but God only knows how.'

Lena laughed. 'Georgia Watkins brought that. Said it was a godsend when hers were babies, but she didn't need it any more. I think she left the instructions around here somewhere...'

She started to search the counter, but Max stopped her. 'We'll look after lunch. I'm starving.'

Luckily, amongst the many boxes, bags and dishes the locals had delivered was a plate of sandwiches and a few bags of crisps. Food that needed no preparation at all was definitely what Lena was looking for.

While Max fixed himself a coffee to replace the one he'd given her, Lena dropped the platter of sandwiches onto the kitchen table. 'Lunch is served!'

'Amazing.' He even sounded as if he meant it. Which, since she imagined that Max Blythe got to eat at the fanciest restaurants in London, was saying something.

Even Willow seemed to understand that food was vital to them all surviving the rest of the day, because she stayed happily staring around herself in her bouncy chair while Lena inhaled the first couple of sandwiches.

'So, along with the food, did we get any real leads on Willow's mother?' Max asked, after long minutes of nothing but the two of them chewing.

Lena recounted everything she'd told Janice, which felt even less optimistic than it had the first time around.

'Sounds like it might take a while, if she doesn't just come forward,' he observed. 'More than twenty-four hours, anyway.'

Lena winced. 'But that doesn't mean it isn't still worth doing. I mean, even if we'd gone straight to the police, do you really think they'd be doing anything more than we are?'

'Willow would be with people who actually know how to look after babies, though.'

'I know how to look after babies,' she snapped, then remembered she'd told him she didn't. Although that had only been because she hated the idea that she *should* know, because she was the woman. With a sigh, she explained. 'I actually took a fostering course last year, and am registered to offer emergency foster care. I haven't had a placement yet, but I know what I should be doing.'

Max surveyed her silently, and Lena tried desperately to figure out what was going on behind those clear, dark eyes. Was he thinking this explained everything? Lonely spinster whose biological clock was ticking tried to hang onto baby that didn't belong to her, that sort of thing?

Except it wasn't that. It wasn't that she wanted a baby of her own, exactly. She just wanted to help.

And she didn't want Willow's mother to go to prison, or have her life ruined, just because she was so scared she couldn't look after a baby on her own, or whatever else had driven her to leaving Willow on Max's doorstep.

After a moment, Max looked away, and reached for another sandwich. 'I called Toby.'

Lena blinked. 'Okay.' She didn't know what that had to do with looking after a baby, but she was hoping he'd explain if she gave him the opportunity.

'I didn't understand why everyone in Wells-on-Water seemed so eager to help a baby whose own mother didn't even want it.'

She sucked in a sharp breath. She hadn't

thought of it from that point of view before. In her head, *of course* Willow's mother loved and wanted her baby, she just didn't think she could look after it. That was why Lena wanted to find and help her.

But in Max's head, Willow's mum had abandoned her because she didn't want her, and that was why she wouldn't come forward and claim her now. Just as his own father had never wanted—or claimed—him.

Why hadn't she seen that before?

'Toby told me that the community here has come a long way since I left,' he went on, still not looking directly at her. 'That it's more supportive, more inclusive now, I guess.'

'I hope so.' Lena's mouth felt dry. How had she not realised how personal this must feel for Max?

'He also told me a lot of that had to do with you.' Now, he looked up, and even if his dark brown eyes were still guarded, she could see the hints of turbulence behind them.

'I…I don't know about that. But I've always loved this village, and the people in it. I know not all of them treated you fairly, or kindly, but they looked after me after my mum died. They supported me. And I guess…I guess I tried to do something to pay that forward to the next generation that lived here.'

'Toby said you were behind basically every community venture of the last decade.'

Lena laughed. 'I don't know about that. But yeah, I've tried to keep involved. Find ways to bring people together.'

Leaning back in his chair, Max stretched his legs out under the kitchen table until they almost brushed against hers. She tucked her ankles under her chair to keep her distance, but she couldn't *quite* banish Janice's suggestions about seduction from her mind.

Serious conversation here, Lena. Not *the time to be playing footsie.*

'Is that why you feel so responsible for Willow? Why you're so worried about the community, and her mother being out there somewhere?'

At least he didn't think she was a lonely spinster, Lena supposed. And it had to be better than telling him the *whole* truth. She wasn't ready for that. Not yet. Maybe not ever.

After all, they were getting along so well. Why ruin it?

'Maybe a bit,' she admitted. 'Mostly I tend to feel responsible for everything, so perhaps this is just a natural extension of that.'

She'd meant it as a joke, but Max's expression turned serious. 'Why do you feel responsible for everything?'

Why? Had she ever even asked *herself* that question? It was just the way it was.

No. That wasn't entirely true. She knew why. It was just that if she delved *too* deep into the why...well, that way lay thoughts and conversations she really didn't want to have with him.

She shrugged, keen to move on, away from her own issues and onto Willow's. 'Guess that's just the way I am.'

He studied her for a moment, perhaps waiting for her to say something more. And when she didn't, he said, 'I remember back when we were in school, walking home one day, across the fields, and running into your brothers.'

Dread bubbled up inside her, the way it always did when someone mentioned an encounter with her brothers—even a decades-old one. The feeling that whispered, *What have they done now?*

'It was the same way I walked every day—we all did, remember?' he went on.

She nodded. The high school was over in Wishcliffe, so every day the kids from Wells-on-Water trudged along the muddy footpath over the fields to get there—rather than take the longer, cleaner route by road.

'And most days your brothers were waiting along the path, under the trees, ready to torment somebody. Sometimes me, but just as often some other poor kid.' There was no emotion in his words, almost as if he were describing something he'd seen in a film, rather than something that had happened to him.

'I'm sorry—' she started, but he cut her off.

'It's not your place to apologise for them. You're not responsible for their actions, not then and certainly not now.'

And Lena *knew* this was true. Intellectually, she knew it. But inside...her subconscious never seemed so sure. She *felt* responsible, even if she shouldn't.

'You were hardly ever on the walk home,' Max said, and she couldn't tell if this was more of the story, or a mitigation for her responsibility.

'Too many clubs at school, or committees for events,' she said, with a wry smile. 'I was always there late, sorting things out, so I'd walk home via the road if it was dark, so I'd have the streetlamps to see by, even though it took longer.'

He nodded. 'That's right. But I remember this one day, you *were* there. And you came across your brothers tormenting me and a friend. This must have been soon after we started at the high school, because it didn't take me too long into my teens to learn to fight back.'

'I remember that part, for sure.' He'd been in constant trouble for fighting at school. No wonder they'd never run in the same circles.

'Anyway, this one day, you stepped right up

into the middle of everything. The crowds gathered around parted for you, and you stood between me and my friend and your brothers, and you told them *stop*.' Max met her gaze and held it. 'And, to everyone's amazement, they did.'

'The one time they ever listened to me, then,' she joked, trying to dismiss the heavy atmosphere that seemed to have filled the kitchen like smoke.

Max shook his head. 'People always listened to you. They still do. You can make people do things they never thought they'd even consider—like taking in an abandoned baby, for instance.'

'You'd have done the same if I wasn't here.'

'I'd have called the police and washed my hands of the whole thing and you know it.'

She did know it. But she still wasn't sure what point Max was trying to make. 'Fine, you would. So?'

'I think that, because people have listened to you for so long, because you were the only person your brothers ever listened to, you feel responsible for them. For everyone in this damned village and probably beyond. But, Lena, the only person you can ever really be responsible for is yourself.'

Max watched as Lena absorbed the idea he'd put out there—that she couldn't be responsible for everything—and dismissed it with a small shake of the head.

'Maybe you're right,' she said, and he knew that there was a 'but' coming. 'But there are things that I *have* taken responsibility for, and gladly.'

'Like Willow.' He wished he understood why she felt so strongly that they should look after the baby. He knew why *he* had come around to that idea, but he couldn't help but feel there was some reason she wasn't telling him that made it matter so much to her.

'Yes, like Willow,' she said. 'But other things, too. Like the community hub.'

'The community hub? What's that?' He knew there hadn't been much time for conversation between looking after Willow and dealing with all the locals, but he was pretty sure she hadn't mentioned that before. Or if she had, he'd been too exhausted to retain the information.

Lena sighed, and looked over at Willow, who was now dozing in her bouncy chair.

No chance of an escape from this conversation there, he thought, mentally thanking whoever had donated the seat. It was definitely Willow's new favourite thing.

'About two years ago, I helped set up a community hub in the old village hall,' Lena explained. 'It was a place for people to come for help and advice, or just some company and a cup of tea. I nagged all sorts of local professionals into donating an hour or two a week there as well. Like, Mr McDonald, who is a retired family law solicitor, and Robbie Jenkins, who runs a home-maintenance firm in Wishcliffe. We had sessions on childcare and parenting, on looking after family finances, even cooking and healthy meal planning. And I got Janice and one of her nurses to run regular drop-in clinics there, including a private family-planning one.'

The sort of clinic that Willow's mum might have gone to for help, Max supposed, when she realised she was pregnant.

'It sounds amazing,' Max said. 'Who paid for it all?'

Lena shrugged. 'We did a lot of fundraising. But they let us use the hall for free, and most people donated their time, or other things. We had a mini-foodbank going at Christmas with another planned for the summer holidays, and a second-hand baby stuff bring and buy sale in the spring.'

'So what happened?' Because he could tell from her voice this story didn't have a happy ending.

'The village hall roof caved in. Right on top of one of our cooking demonstrations.'

Max winced. 'Is it being fixed?'

'I don't know. I guess that will be up to the new owners.' Getting to her feet, Lena paced across to the sink and began rinsing out their coffee cups and plates.

'The village is selling the hall?'

'It was deemed unsafe—which, I mean, nobody could really argue with that after the roof collapse. But it turned out that the roof was only the start of it. There was so much that needed fixing up...there was no way we could raise the money for it. So the village council decided to sell it, and put the proceeds aside for other community ventures.'

'Another hub?'

'Maybe. Except there's plenty of groups around here that deserve a share of that money, and whatever we get it won't be enough to buy or even rent another base of operations for the hub, not within the village anyway. We're a picturesque seaside village, Max. If you don't think half the buildings around here are holiday lets these days you haven't been paying attention.'

He hadn't, he realised. He'd been so busy thinking about what returning to Wells-on-Water meant to him, he hadn't even noticed all the changes within the village.

'That's why you started the hub,' he said, finally beginning to understand. 'To give the real locals a place that still felt like theirs.'

'In part,' Lena admitted. 'But also because… there aren't so many opportunities around here, you know that. People who choose to stay do it because they love this place more than the money they could earn elsewhere—or because they don't have many opportunities wherever they go.'

'And you brought both those sorts of people together, to see if they could help each other.'

'That's the idea. Or it was.' Lena's shoulders slumped over the sink as she stared out of the back window over the grounds of the Manor House.

Max had more questions he wanted to ask about the hub, but he sensed that Lena's mood was diving fast just talking about it, so he decided to save them for later. Plus, he had an idea or two that he wanted to test out before he mentioned them to her. No point raising her hopes if he couldn't pull off what he wanted to promise.

'It really does seem like a different village from the one I left behind,' he said. 'And I think Toby's right. A lot of that has to do with you. You should be proud of everything you've done for this place. I have no idea where you even found the time, let alone the energy.'

She turned at that and gave him a tired smile. 'Well, when it's something worthwhile…' Her gaze slid away towards Willow. Another worthwhile project she'd taken on, he supposed.

'Toby had a suggestion about Willow, you know.' The words were out before he could decide if it was a good idea to say them. Until the moment he spoke he honestly hadn't been sure if he was going to share his half-brother's thoughts with Lena—let alone go along with them.

Now…now it felt almost inevitable.

She'd done so much for this place in the sixteen years since he ran away. Now he was back, the least he could do was back her up a bit. Wasn't it?

Even if the idea still scared him stupid.

'He had an idea who her mother might be?' Lena asked.

Max shook his head. 'No. No…it was something else. He agreed with me that we needed to contact the authorities.'

'Max—' she started to interrupt, but he held up a hand and, with a mutinous glare, she let him finish.

'But he pointed out that since the note Willow's mum left behind seems to hint that I am the father, and especially now you've told me you actually have foster-care training, perhaps those authorities—with a good word from Janice, maybe—might be willing to leave Willow with us a little longer, under their supervision, while we try and sort all this out?'

Lena's brow creased into a confused frown. 'But you're *not* the father.'

'No.' That much, at least, he was sure of.

'And you'd let everyone around here believe that you might be—that you got some girl in trouble and abandoned her?'

He shrugged, as if that idea didn't bother him—even though the very thought made his chest tight. He wouldn't do that, and he knew it. That would have to be enough.

And maybe it was a little bit of punishment, for leaving Lena and never checking up after their first time together. If she *had* been pregnant… well, that was exactly what he would have done, even if it would have been unintentional.

'It's not like they don't all already think the worst of me. We can say we're waiting on a DNA test or something.'

'But this is your fresh start,' Lena argued. 'Your chance to show everyone around here who you really are. Who you can be.'

The idea of reclaiming his reputation, of proving all the gossips of Wells-on-Water wrong, still glittered in the corner of his mind. But Willow mattered more. And so did Lena. She deserved to not have *all* that responsibility on her shoulders for a change. He could share the load, couldn't he?

It's the right thing to do, his mother's voice whispered in his brain.

'I've still got the Manor House,' he said flippantly. 'And the rest of it? Who cares what they all think, anyway?'

'You do,' Lena said, more astutely than he liked.

'Not any more,' he lied, his voice firm.

She studied him carefully for a long moment, and he schooled his expression to give no hint of his real thoughts. Finally, she nodded.

'Then we'll call Janice in the morning and see what she thinks.'

'You don't want to do it now?' he asked, surprised.

Lena shook her head. 'Let's wait out our twenty-four hours, first. Maybe some information will turn up on the mother before then, and you won't need to lie.'

'Maybe,' Max echoed. But he knew as well as she did that it was a long shot.

As she turned away to check on Willow, he realised what she was doing: giving him an out. Time to change his mind.

But he knew he wouldn't take it. He needed to do this. For Willow, for Lena—and for the boy he'd been, all those years ago.

He couldn't change his past in this village. But he could help Lena change its future.

* * *

Willow wouldn't stop crying.

Holding her against her shoulder, Lena crooned softly to the baby, hoping that a song might soothe her as it had earlier that day, but it didn't seem to be doing any good. She'd been wailing since dinner time, and she showed no sign of stopping any time soon.

After doing his own shift walking Willow up and down the length of the house trying to soothe her, Max had gone to deal with a few emails in his study. Leaving Lena to pace around the drawing room, dodging all the baby stuff that the village had donated to help with looking after Willow. None of which had seemed to be any help this evening.

She'd changed her nappy, fed her, winded her, checked her temperature was okay…and nothing seemed to be making a bit of difference. Lena had even flicked through the relevant chapters of the books Janice had left, and the online forums she'd bookmarked that morning, but none of them had any more useful advice than waiting it out.

Babies cry. It's what they do. It doesn't mean I'm doing this wrong.

It felt as if she was, though. God, how did new mothers cope with this? The complete helplessness in the face of a squalling infant who didn't seem to want anything but to cry?

'My turn.' Max's voice came from the doorway. 'You need some sleep.'

She shook her head. 'I can do a bit longer.'

'It's gone midnight, Lena.' He moved closer, holding out his arms for the baby. 'Let someone help you for a change, yeah?'

The thought was such a strange one, she stopped and stared. Oh, people helped her all the time—when she asked them for help. Like this morning with the stuff for Willow, or Janice bringing her clothes.

But the idea of someone else seeing what she needed and stepping in to give it to her without her having to ask? That one was new.

If she weren't so tired and her head weren't pounding from listening to Willow scream for the last hour, she might object to Max assuming he knew what she needed. Or she'd point out that the baby was every bit as much his responsibility as hers, if not more. As it was…

'Thank you,' she said, and placed Willow in his arms. Then, impulsively, she kissed him on the cheek and made a dash for the stairs.

She was still overthinking that kiss as she lay in bed in the guest room half an hour later, Willow's screams muffled but still clearly audible from below. It had just been a friendly thank-you kiss, nothing she wouldn't give to any other friend who helped her out.

Even if, being that close to him, the very scent of his skin had threatened to overpower her exhaustion and lead her thoughts down a path that had nothing to do with sleep or childcare…

Did he feel it, too, being close to her? That tug of a connection between them that had never quite disappeared, even after so many years? Maybe it was just because he'd been her first. Or because he'd grown up so damn well she couldn't help but wonder how it would be between them now. But whatever the reason, she had to admit that she wasn't only looking at Max as a carer for Willow.

She must have dozed off eventually, still wrestling with her thoughts about the man whose house she was staying in. But she jerked awake again not long after, Willow's cries suddenly nearer.

Swinging her legs slowly over the side of the bed, she padded to the door, and found Max in the hallway.

'Sorry,' he said. 'I thought I'd finally got her settled in her basket, so popped down to grab a glass of water.'

Lena shook her tired head. 'It's okay. She's really unsettled tonight, huh?'

'Seems so.' He gave her a weary smile. 'Go on, you head back to bed.'

But she didn't. Pushing gently past Max, she made her way into his room, and lifted Willow from her basket. The baby settled a little in her arms, at least.

'Worried I've done something stupid to upset her?' Max stood in the doorway, his arms folded across his broad chest.

'No.' Her exhausted legs were about to give way, so Lena dropped to sit on the edge of his bed. 'But we're in this together, right? And it looks like it's going to be a long night.'

'What do you suggest, then?' Max moved to sit beside her on the bed, and they both stared down at Willow's tiny face.

'She's happier being held,' Lena said, thinking back to everything she'd read in Janice's books. 'But I'm worried that if I try to sit up with her I'll fall asleep—and so would you,' she added before he could argue. 'And I don't want to be dashing back and forth between two rooms all night.'

'So we take turns?' Max suggested. 'Stay here while she settles, so we can both keep an eye on her and doze in between. And if we're lucky, maybe she'll fall deeply enough asleep to put her in the basket eventually.'

'Sounds like the best plan we've had so far,'

Lena admitted. Holding Willow to her chest with one arm, she used the other to lever herself up the bed until her back rested against the headboard. She adjusted the baby in her arms, as Max manoeuvred the duvet from under her legs to cover her.

Then he settled himself on the other side of the bed. 'You okay with her for now?' he asked.

Lena nodded. 'Try and get a nap while she's quiet,' she suggested. 'Because when she starts crying again, it's your turn.'

'Fair enough.' Max's words were muffled against his pillow as he lay down on his side, facing them. 'Night, Lena. Night, Willow.'

She looked down at his dark hair against the white sheets, his face peaceful but exhausted, and grinned, despite her tiredness.

This really isn't how I imagined getting Max Blythe into bed again.

CHAPTER SEVEN

MAX WOKE TO SILENCE, which seemed unexpected, and a warm body in his arms, which was even more so. He opened his eyes slowly as he tried to make sense of the world.

He was lying down in bed, that much was clear, and he vaguely remembered Willow settling into a deep enough sleep that he'd risked putting her in her basket. That must have been—he squinted at the clock on his bedside table—two hours ago. He lifted his head a little more to check, and saw her small body still in there, the light blanket over her rising and falling with her tiny breaths. Still sleeping. Wow, that might be a record.

He turned his attention back to the bed.

Blonde hair over his pillow, and a pale arm thrown across his chest.

Lena Phillips is in my bed.

Oh, and didn't that just raise all sorts of interesting possibilities?

Now his brain had caught up with his body, he knew full well why she was there—and it hadn't had anything to do with a late-night seduction. But his body didn't seem to care. All it knew was that a beautiful woman was lying next to him. No, not just a beautiful woman. *Lena.*

Lena Phillips was in his bed, and that was taking his brain—not just his body—down all sorts of interesting side paths.

Not that he intended to try and do anything about them. For one, Willow was still in the room, and bound to wake up at any moment. And for another…he and Lena had history. And they also had a future—at least for the next few days. They had to focus on Willow and finding her family.

Muddying the waters by doing anything about the sexual tension between them wouldn't help.

Right?

Max sighed. He was going to have to keep working on convincing himself of that, apparently.

Lena's eyelids fluttered, then opened, and she blinked up at him. As he watched, he saw the initial confusion in her eyes fade, replaced by something else. Heat. Want. The same things he'd felt on realising their position on waking.

Then she pulled away, an apologetic smile

on her lips, and he knew that she'd just gone through the same mental gymnastics that he had, and apparently reached the same conclusion.

They couldn't take this any further while they had Willow to take care of.

The only problem with that logic, Max realised, was that once Willow was gone—hopefully safely back with her family—he'd be going back to London. And he really hadn't planned on spending much time in Wells-on-Water after that.

Lena belonged here, and he never had. And Max had enough trouble making time for girlfriends in the same city as him to believe that there was any hope of anything longer distance.

No, if they *did* try to make something of this, Max knew it would end the same way it had last time—with him driving away and leaving Lena to the life she deserved.

Except this time I'll leave a number, just in case.

On cue, Willow let out a small whimper, followed by a louder cry. Peace and rest were over.

Lena sat up against the headboard, and yawned. 'Well, at least we all got *some* sleep last night.'

Swinging his legs over the side of the bed, Max reached into Willow's basket and lifted her out. 'More than I'd dared hoped for at the start of the night.'

The baby settled against his chest as he sat back down on the bed, and he wondered when this had become natural to him. Not easy, for certain, and he was still sure he was going to mess it up every second of the day. But holding a baby, something he'd never done before this week, now felt perfectly normal.

As did having Lena in his home. In his bed.

'So, what's the plan for the day?' Lena asked.

Glancing over, he saw that she was worrying her lower lip with her teeth as she waited for his answer, and realised what she was really asking. Did he still want to go ahead with their plan from the day before: pretending he *could* be Willow's dad, so they could keep looking after her while they searched for her mum?

Did he?

He knew it was a risk. It could be a huge hit to his reputation here, which had always been a bit tattered to start with. If he *had* hoped to come back and make a life here in Wells-on-Water, people gossiping about how he'd knocked up some poor girl then abandoned her wouldn't make that easy. And if the truth came out, he knew people would find a way to doubt his motives, perhaps suggesting he was using Willow to get Lena into bed, or something. Which he wasn't, despite current evidence.

And if the police found out he'd lied about possibly being the father, he didn't even know if there would be penalties for that.

But none of that changed a damn thing. He was doing it anyway.

'Well, I guess we'd better get things in motion with social services,' he said. 'And figure out what our story is going to be, if we want to keep this one with us a little longer.'

Lena's smile lit up the whole room, more so than the summer sun outside the window.

She jumped out of bed. 'In that case, you change Willow, and I'll go make up her bottle—and get the coffee machine going. And then we can call Janice and figure out how to do this.'

'Sounds good,' Max replied. 'Because this is definitely going to require coffee.'

Janice thought Max's—or Toby's—plan was a great idea. Lena knew her friend had been uncomfortable not notifying the proper people in the first place, and at least this way they were nominally following proper procedure.

'I'll make the calls,' Janice said eagerly, when she called. 'You guys sit tight.'

Which meant that, until Willow woke from her post-breakfast nap in what Lena was privately calling the Chair of Joy, there was nothing to do but sit around with Max, drinking coffee, and wondering how he felt about their… rather cuddly wake up that morning.

She knew how she had felt. She'd felt a little embarrassed, worried about her morning breath, guilty for forgetting about Willow for a long moment as she'd stared at him, and…

Well. Mostly she'd just wished that circumstances were different and she'd been able to take advantage of the situation. In fact, if Willow hadn't woken up just then, she couldn't say for sure that she wouldn't have.

There was just something magnetic about the way he looked at her. How he made her feel—as if her whole body had come alive despite its ongoing exhaustion.

Did he feel the same? What would have happened the other night when she'd brought him back to the Manor House if there *hadn't* been a baby on the doorstep…?

But there had been. And they still had to deal with that.

He'd been the one to insist she call Janice and go ahead with their plan.

Which brought her back to the question of why he was doing this.

He didn't want to be looking after Willow, she knew that. He'd admitted that if she weren't there, he would have handed her over to the police in a heartbeat.

So why? Had all that talk about responsibility shamed him into it?

Or was it something else…?

She'd been carefully ignoring the tiny corner of her mind that suggested he might be doing it to spend more time with her. Quite apart from the fact that he'd shown no indication that he was looking for a repeat of their last night together since the moment they'd found Willow on the doorstep—although before was up for debate—it was doing Max a disservice to think that way.

But that was before she'd woken up in his arms to find him watching her sleep, a heat she remembered well simmering behind his eyes. Maybe the chance to get her into bed wasn't *why* he was doing this—especially since so far sleep was far higher up the priority list than anything else they might be doing between the sheets—but she got the impression that it could be a pretty great added bonus.

For both of them.

She shook the thought away, forcing herself to face reality. If sex was really what he wanted, she was pretty sure he could find that anywhere he wanted. The fact that he hadn't sought it out in so long—long enough that he could be so sure that Willow wasn't his…well, she had to admit, that had come as a surprise.

But one they wouldn't be sharing with social services, if they wanted their plan to work.

They talked about it again, as they waited for Janice to arrive—over lunch, and into the afternoon, between taking care of Willow. They had a plan. They wouldn't mention Max's imaginary ex-partner if they could help it, just say that he wanted to preserve her privacy but, since he hadn't been aware she might be pregnant, wanted to alert the proper authorities in case this was some sort of scam.

Of course, that plan fell apart the moment the social worker Janice had called, accompanied by a representative from the local police force, finally arrived and started asking questions.

'Obviously our main concern is for the mother's safety,' Constable Robbins said, his bored tone suggesting that, actually, his main concern was getting all this sorted so he could forget about it. 'Normally with an abandoned baby we'd be doing appeals and all sorts. But you say the baby could be yours?' This last was added with a raise of the eyebrows that insinuated all sorts of things Lena didn't really like.

'The mother left a note suggesting that,' Lena said. 'That's one of the reasons we're so keen to keep Willow here with us until she's found.'

'Surely you must have some idea who she is, then?' Sarah, the social worker, asked Max. 'If you could give us her name, or, well, a list of names, I suppose, then perhaps we could track her down for you?' She was blushing now, poor thing. Lena supposed that Max's glower at the suggestion of his leaving a trail of pregnant women behind him was sort of intimidating if you didn't know how horribly embarrassed he must be by this whole thing.

'As I said at the start, I have not been contacted by any past…acquaintance to tell me of a pregnancy. And obviously, as this is a very sensitive matter, I would like to make contact personally to try and sort this out. Given my public standing, a DNA test will of course be required. Really, we were only alerting you as a courtesy in case it emerges that this is simply an attempt by a desperate woman to play off my wealth.' Hiding the lie within the truth, Lena thought. Of course he hadn't been contacted by anyone, because there was no one to contact him. Which meant those phone calls he was promising to try and track down Willow's mother were a blatant lie.

Lena watched Max's face as he spoke, the clipped, almost aristocratic tones clearly designed to end the discussion then and there. She could imagine him using such tactics and intimidation in the boardroom, negotiating deals and getting things done. And glancing over at Sarah and Constable Robbins, she could see that it was working. Sarah was already packing up her paperwork.

But underneath it, she could see the faint signs of stress in the lines around Max's mouth, the set of his jaw. He was hating this. Hating lying. Hating trashing his reputation this way.

And she started to wonder if he really was all that different from the boy she'd connected with on that last day of school, so long ago. If everything that had happened since—and maybe before, now she thought about it—had simply been a shield he'd built up. A mask made to help him survive in a world that had treated him unfairly for so long.

She'd seen the mask slip just once in all the years she'd known him.

She wondered now if she could make it slip again.

Janice, who'd accompanied them to ensure things went smoothly, hurried things along at that point, getting everything tied up for now and everyone who didn't belong there out of the house far faster than Lena thought she could have managed. In lots of ways the doctor had the same sort of authority Max exuded, except hers felt more natural, born out of years of study and more years of dealing with people every day, often when they needed someone to tell them what was wrong and what to do next.

And then, it was just Lena, Max and Willow at the Manor House again, left with nothing but a promise of a return visit from Sarah very soon to 'see how they were doing' and a reminder from Constable Robbins to get in touch if there were 'any developments'.

Lena sagged against the door as she closed it behind them. Max had Willow in his arms again, humming tunelessly to her as he paced the length of the large hallway, trying to soothe her. And suddenly it hit her, exactly what they'd agreed to here.

'What if we don't find the mother?' Her words seemed too loud in the almost empty house. 'What happens then?'

Max reached the end of the hall and turned to start back again, looking up from Willow's face to meet Lena's gaze with his dark, unreadable one. 'You'll find her. I have faith in you.'

Lena just wished she had the same faith in herself.

But faith counted for nothing if she didn't keep moving. Action was what mattered; she'd always known that. Ever since her mother died, and she became somehow responsible for a family of men, far too young.

'It's getting late already.' She pushed away from the door and started towards the kitchen. 'We should eat. I think someone left some sort of pasta bake we can just shove in the oven for dinner.'

'Sounds perfect,' Max replied.

They tried to put Willow back in the Chair of Joy while they ate, but she was having none of it

'I don't get it,' Max said, frustrated, as he picked her up again. 'She's clean, she's eaten, she's burped, she's slept…what else is there to want when you're this little?'

Lena gave a small smile. 'The same thing we all want. Connection.' Max looked puzzled, so she explained. 'Her eyesight is still very, very limited, remember. If she's over there and we're here, she can't see us. And right now, I guess she wants to know that she's not alone.'

Max looked back down at the baby in his arms with a softness Lena knew not many would expect from him. 'Well, okay, then,' he said, and proceeded to eat his entire meal one-handed, cuddling Willow throughout, even after she fell asleep in his arms.

'Do you want me to take the first shift with her tonight so you can get some sleep?' Lena asked as they loaded the dishwasher. Max had proved surprisingly adept at doing things one-handed, now he understood why it was necessary.

'No. You sleep,' he said. 'She's comfy enough here, anyway.'

'She certainly looks it.' Lena wondered what it said about her that she was almost jealous of Willow, who got to have Max's arms around her while Lena was going to bed alone.

Probably it said nothing more than, as she'd told Max, everyone wanted, needed connection. And it had been a long time since she'd had any. Max wasn't the only one who'd been through a bit of a dry spell lately.

She could always suggest they try the same tactic as last night, sharing the bed to share the load of looking after Willow...but she didn't want to sound needy. Or give him the idea that she was angling for more than just his help with the baby here. If he thought she was getting Ideas about them, he could call that social worker right back and tell her the truth—that Willow couldn't be his.

No. She should try to keep some sort of distance between them, at least for now. Until they got everything with Willow sorted out. She didn't want the heightened emotions of the situation to get them both tangled up in something neither of them had really planned for.

A second one-night stand, the night of the

party, would have been one thing. But they were friends now, she hoped. And that meant anything that happened between them had consequences.

Like her having to tell him the truth about what happened sixteen years ago.

And she really wasn't ready for that.

Lena glanced at the clock on the wall: just gone nine o'clock. She'd never normally be in bed this early but right now she felt as if she could barely keep her eyes open.

'Go on,' Max said. 'You go up.'

'You'll come get me when you need to swap?'

'You bet I will,' he replied, with a smile. 'I'll see you in a few hours, yeah?'

Lena nodded, and turned to leave, before stopping suddenly and swinging back—something Max clearly hadn't anticipated, as he was right behind her, one arm raised to shut the door.

She managed to avoid crashing into him and the baby, but only just. And as it was, it put them closer than they'd been since they found Willow. Close enough that she could feel the warmth radiating from him and the bundle in his arms.

Willow was tucked in the crook of his left arm, his right resting against the doorframe above her head. And all Lena could think was that she was so close she could kiss him, if she wanted. If he wanted.

If he weren't holding a baby right now.

She blinked, and shook her head.

'Lena? You okay?' Max asked softly, and she nodded.

'Yeah. I just…' What was it she'd wanted to tell him? Why had she turned back?

The words came to her in a rush, and she looked up from his lips to meet his warm gaze instead.

'I just wanted to tell you that you're a really good man.'

She half expected him to laugh, to knock the compliment away with a joke about sleep deprivation or something. And she thought he almost expected that, too. But maybe they were both too tired to bother with that sort of thing any more.

Instead, his lips curved up into a slight smile, and he whispered, 'Thank you.'

And, God, she wanted to kiss him. But instead, she turned on her heel and ran for bed.

Max couldn't sleep. Which was ridiculous, because he was so far beyond exhausted. He'd finally given in and woken Lena up around three, when Willow had stirred for yet another feed. He'd moved the Moses basket into the guest room while Lena fed the baby, and refused to let himself dwell on how much easier this would be if they just shared his bed again tonight.

He needed actual sleep, and a wall between him and the crying baby. That was only sensible.

So he'd collapsed into bed in his blissfully silent bedroom certain that he'd be dead to the world until morning.

Except…

Except he couldn't get that moment out of his head. That brief few seconds when he'd honestly believed that Lena Phillips was about to kiss him. Again.

Instead, she'd told him he was a good man—which was absurd, because nobody had ever called him that before. A good negotiator, sure. A good businessman even. But he'd never been a good son, or a good friend, and certainly not a good boyfriend.

A good man?

It had to be the sleep deprivation talking.

But…he'd felt the truth of her words in his heart as she'd spoken, and known she believed them, even if he wasn't at all sure he did.

He told himself she was just grateful that he'd bought them more time to find Willow's mum. But that just brought him back to why he'd done that in the first place.

He wanted to pretend it was to keep Lena with him until they could finish what he'd hoped they'd been about to start the night of

Finn and Victoria's party. But that would be a lie—especially since looking after a tiny baby who didn't sleep was objectively *not* conducive to seduction. If he'd tried to take Lena to bed tonight he was pretty sure that one of them would have fallen asleep before they'd even got their clothes off.

He'd done it because it was the right thing to do. Maybe his mother's ghost had been whispering in his ear—not that he believed in such things. But being back in Wells-on-Water, he had to admit that her memory felt closer than ever.

And more than anything, his mum had believed in doing the right thing, not the easy one.

Well, he hoped she'd be happy at his choices since he'd come back to the Manor House. Looking after Willow was not easy. And he had a feeling that resisting Lena's charms while the baby was in the house wouldn't be easy, either.

Finally, sleep must have claimed him because the next thing he knew it was morning, the sun was up, and he could hear Lena moving something heavy downstairs.

Bracing himself for another home invasion, he showered and dressed quickly before heading down, only to find the hallway empty except for an ancient-looking, huge-wheeled pram.

He peered into it and found Willow staring

up at him. She didn't look any surer about this turn of events than he felt.

'Isn't it gorgeous?' Lena appeared from the kitchen, two travel coffee mugs in hand. 'I think Mrs Jenkins has been keeping it in her garage since her own kids were babies, hoping there'd be grandchildren one day who'd need it.'

'Are we sure it was just for her babies?' Max looked critically at the metal frame, but even he had to admit it was polished to perfection. 'Not, say, the last eight generations of her family? The thing looks positively Victorian.' If it had come from Mrs Hillary Jenkins, into his home, there was also the chance it could be booby-trapped to maim or injure him, although he didn't mention that to Lena. Mrs Jenkins had been…whatever the absolute opposite of his number one fan was, all through his youth.

'These prams are all the rage again these days, according to Victoria,' Lena replied. 'The originals go for silly money on Internet auction sites.'

'Maybe for social media photos,' Max allowed. 'But what are they like to actually push?'

'That's what we're going to find out,' Lena said brightly. 'We're going for a walk.'

'We as in…?'

'As in you, too. Come on.'

It seemed easier to go along with Lena's plans

than argue, especially since she held the coffee hostage until they were outside. Together, they carefully manoeuvred the pram down the front steps and over the gravel until they hit the road into the village.

'Isn't it a beautiful day?' Lena took a deep breath of the summer air and beamed.

'How much coffee have you had already?' He knew she'd been up at least on and off since three, and yet she looked as fresh as the proverbial daisy.

'Lots,' she answered honestly. 'I'm scheduling in a crash mid-afternoon for a nap, so prepare to be on Willow duty then.'

'Fair enough.' At some point, he was going to have to get back to actual work, but it didn't look as though that was going to be today. He'd managed to respond to the odd urgent email, and send a message to his assistant to postpone meetings and take care of anything non-business-critical that came up, but that was about all. Besides, he wasn't sure he trusted his judgement when he was this tired.

It was ridiculous, really, he decided as they strolled down the hill towards the rooftops and warm stone buildings of Wells-on-Water. When he was working on a big project, or in time-sensitive negotiations, he frequently functioned on less sleep than he'd had over the last couple of days.

The difference, he supposed, was that time was then his own. Once the crisis was over, he could crash. He could hand over responsibility and sleep until he was refreshed. Or even take a weekend off to chill out at some resort somewhere, with or without company.

Here, with Lena and Willow, the sleep he did get was broken by her cries and, more importantly, the constant need to try and interpret her desires. Even when she was with Lena, he never felt fully off duty. If she was in the house, he felt responsible for her.

That was the exhausting part. God, how did parents do it? He was in awe.

More and more, as the days went on, he was coming to understand how a scared, desperate, presumably single and maybe young mother could feel that her only option was to pass that responsibility on to an adult. One with resources she, perhaps, didn't have.

Money makes everything easier.

He'd known that since he was a child, watching his father's family living in a mansion in Wishcliffe, while his mother worked two jobs to keep them housed and fed. It was one of the reasons he'd left Wells-on-Water as a teen, determined to seek his fortune and build a different life for them.

That his mother hadn't lived long enough to really enjoy it still hurt.

But it hadn't occurred to him to use his money to try and fix this. Even Lena had called in favours and support rather than ordering new things, which he could easily have done. He could have called an agency, found a nanny, anything. But he hadn't.

Willow wasn't something he could throw money at to solve the problems that had brought her to his door. Not entirely, anyway.

Lena was right. The community was what mattered here.

If only it weren't one that had completely alienated him before he'd even turned eighteen.

The fields either side of the road gave way to houses, then shops, and then the familiar sight of the cross at the centre of the village, a memorial to those lost in the wars. Max had driven through the village since he'd arrived, but not spent much time looking around. Now, he took a moment to absorb the changes.

Some shops had changed hands, that was obvious, although Mrs Jenkins's corner shop still had pride of place by the cross. The church had new, more modern signs outside, which clashed with the ancient stones and the stained-glass windows. The pub opposite—the one Lena's dad had owned and operated—looked a little run-down around the edges, which surprised him. Maybe the family had sold it—hadn't Victoria mentioned something about Lena managing the King's Arms in Wishcliffe, now? He couldn't imagine Lena letting it get into such a state.

He turned his attention back to the streets around him. There were bins at regular intervals, which sorted recyclables from non-recyclables—something Max would bet large amounts of money Lena was behind. And there, at the far end of the village, he could just make out the village hall, the roof covered in scaffolding and canvas.

'Is it as you remember?' Lena asked softly.

'Mostly.' He turned his attention back to the pram he was pushing. For an antique, it moved surprisingly smoothly. Inside, Willow lay peacefully tucked up under a white crocheted blanket. 'She's asleep. Shall we see if anywhere will serve us breakfast?'

It was still early, but the cafe diagonally across from the corner shop was open, and the smell of frying bacon and freshly brewed coffee was enticing. Max wasn't at all surprised when, upon entering, Lena was greeted as an old friend by the girl behind the counter, and a man emerged from the kitchen in a greasy apron to hug her welcome.

'I wondered if we'd see you today, love,' he said, in a broad accent Max couldn't quite identify. 'I remember when my three were that age, some mornings all I needed was someone else to make me breakfast. No, don't bother with menus. I'll just bring you two of everything. That's what you need—a proper plateful.'

He disappeared back into the kitchen, and Lena guided them to a table in the corner where they could park the pram up against the wall without blocking any of the passageways between tables. The girl from the counter placed two giant mugs of tea on the table before they'd even sat down.

'You're a regular here, I take it?' Max asked Lena with raised eyebrows.

'Oh, everyone in the village knows Lena!' The girl flashed them both a grin. 'It just makes a change to be helping her out, that's all.'

She disappeared back to her post as the door opened and another customer came in. Max took a moment to savour his tea in silence—until a shadow covered their table, and he looked up to see one of the banes of his younger self's existence standing over him.

Mrs Hillary Jenkins herself.

CHAPTER EIGHT

EVERY VILLAGE HAD a Hillary Jenkins, Lena was sure of it.

Somewhere between her sixties and her eighties—Lena wouldn't dare try to guess which—Mrs Jenkins had steel-grey hair, tightly curled against her head, and wore the sort of dresses in thick floral material Lena didn't even know where to buy. She also had the biggest mouth of anyone Lena had ever met.

On her most charitable days, she reminded herself that while Mrs Jenkins's three children had left the village and not looked back, and her husband had run away to Southampton with a primary school teacher twenty years ago, Mrs Jenkins's devotion to Wells-on-Water and its community never wavered.

On her bad days, she muttered to herself that Hillary Jenkins was a gossiping busybody who cared more about catching someone doing something wrong than doing anything right herself.

Today was somewhere in the middle, but, since Willow was currently snoozing away in the pram that Mrs Jenkins herself had donated, Lena forced herself to smile and be charming—just in case Max went the other way. From what she remembered of their youth, and his comments earlier, she wasn't sure that Max and Mrs Jenkins had ever had the best relationship.

'Hillary! How lovely to see you.' Lena started to her feet, but Mrs Jenkins put a hand on her shoulder and pushed her back down.

'Don't you be standing on my account, Lena.' The glare she shot Max's way suggested that he should have considered it, though. 'You need to rest when you can, with a baby to look after.'

Another pointed look at Max. Lena suspected that the story about Max perhaps being Willow's father was fully doing the rounds, then. Well, he couldn't say she hadn't warned him.

'Honestly, Hillary, I'm just helping out. Max is doing all the really hard work.'

'Hmm.' Mrs Jenkins didn't look entirely convinced, but her demeanour softened ever so slightly, which Lena decided to call a victory. 'I've always said that men needed to help out more around here.'

'The beautiful pram you lent us has certainly helped with that,' Max said smoothly. 'Willow loves being taken for walks in it so much she's already fallen asleep. And it's in such good condition.'

'Well, I do believe in looking after things,' Mrs Jenkins admitted. 'And helping out where I can, of course. Speaking of which…'

She turned and motioned towards another woman by the counter, who'd presumably come in with her. It took Lena a moment to place her, only because she wasn't someone she was used to seeing hanging around with Hillary Jenkins.

'Hello, Margery,' Lena said, smiling as the woman approached. 'Max, this is Margery Griffiths. She moved here after your time, and she runs the craft shop down opposite the village hall.'

Margery, with her long boho dresses, brightly hennaed hair, and clinking silver jewellery, was often the subject of Hillary's rants about the nature of the occupants of Wells-on-Water. Apparently, all that hippy-dippy home-made stuff could only be bad for the village. Lena suspected she was worried about her profits at the corner store if everyone started making their own jam.

But apparently the two of them had now teamed up together. Which made her nervous.

'Now. Lena. We know you're always doing a lot for this village, but taking on a baby single-handed goes above and beyond.' Hillary didn't even look at Max as she spoke, but Lena saw him roll his eyes at her exclusion of him from the narrative.

'Honestly, I wanted to do it,' Lena said. 'And Max has been doing most of it anyway. I'm just helping.'

'As he should,' Margery muttered under her breath. Yeah, the fake news that Max might be the father had definitely spread around the village. Lena didn't know *how* she was going to fix that.

'Well, there's no shame in asking for help,' Hillary went on. 'But since we know you never do, we're going to insist. Margery and I will be at the Manor House at seven o'clock this evening to babysit this little mite, while you two go out for dinner.'

'Roberto is already holding his best table for you,' Margery added. 'So you can't say no.'

Lena met Max's gaze across the table. He gave an almost imperceptible shrug, as if to say, *It's up to you.*

Dinner. With Max. Almost like…a date. Was this Hillary and Margery setting them up? Had they decided that seducing Max and looking after his possible baby was the only way Lena was ever going to get the happily ever after they'd decided she deserved?

Possibly. Or perhaps they were intending for her to rehabilitate him from his rakish ways, or something. That sounded more likely.

Did she even *want* to go out to dinner? Well, no. She wanted to curl up in her pyjamas and eat takeaway Chinese, as she always did.

But she *did* want to spend time with Max. Away from Willow, much as she adored the small girl. Time for just the two of them, to figure out where they might have ended up the other night if it hadn't been for a basket on the doorstep of the Manor House. Maybe even to talk about everything that had passed for the two of them since that night in the back of his old car, sixteen years ago.

Well, maybe not *everything*.

But a chance to figure out who they were now, and what that meant, now he was back.

Maybe nothing. But perhaps…

Lena smiled up at Hillary and Margery. 'That would be wonderful, and so very kind of you. Thank you for thinking of us.'

The two women beamed matching smiles. 'Then we'll leave you to your breakfast and see you at seven.'

As they headed for the door, Lena realised she was going to have to go home and find something suitable to wear for a date with Max Blythe.

Breakfast proved to be the biggest meal Max had ever eaten in his life—and he enjoyed every mouthful.

'You're always hungrier when you're tired,' Lena said, knowledgeably, when he commented on it.

'Guess we'd better skip lunch, if we're going out for dinner.' Two large meals in one day was plenty for a guy who often forgot to eat between meetings if his secretary wasn't nagging him. And really, he must call into work…later.

Max was sort of surprised that Lena had agreed to the dinner in the first place, but not nearly as surprised as he was that Hillary Jenkins had offered, even when she clearly thought he was some feckless father who had abandoned a pregnant girl.

'Are we sure that going out for dinner is a good idea?' he asked. It seemed unlikely that Hillary Jenkins wouldn't have *some* sort of ulterior motive for the offer, even if he was finding it hard to imagine what it could be.

'Don't you want to?' Lena asked.

He swung his gaze to hers and saw the uncertainty there. Did she really think he was still the guy who ran out on her after their first time together?

'Of course I want to,' he said, with feeling. 'A whole evening with you, without the interruptions of nappy changes and feeds? It sounds brilliant.'

Lena's expression relaxed. 'Then you're worried about leaving Willow with Hillary and Margery?'

Yeah, that sounded better than 'I think this might all be a cunning ploy to destroy me somehow.' 'Something like that.'

'It's sweet that you're worrying.' Smiling, she reached across the table to place a hand on his, and Max felt electricity shoot up his arm at their connection. 'But I think they'll be okay. Hillary is one of the go-to babysitters for basically everybody in the village.'

'Poor kids,' Max muttered under his breath, making Lena laugh. 'Well, I guess we're going out to dinner, then.'

'I guess we are. But I need to go home first,' Lena said. 'Janice brought me some basics yesterday, but if I'm going to be staying with Willow and you at the Manor House any longer, I'm going to need my own stuff. Not to mention something suitable for Roberto's tonight.'

'Is it fancy there?' The poshest place to eat in Wells-on-Water when Max had lived there had been the sit-in fish and chip shop.

'Fancier than everywhere else,' Lena replied. 'It's a proper, family-run Italian restaurant. I think you'll like it.'

'I'm sure I will.' Especially if it meant spending an evening with Lena, with no distractions.

How could he not?

* * *

But by seven o'clock, the whole plan seemed in jeopardy.

Lena had left Max with Willow for an hour or so while she drove back to her cottage and packed, and after an initial existential panic about being left completely alone with a child, without supervision, Max had actually managed perfectly well for the first forty-five minutes. It was only the last quarter of an hour that went to hell.

First, he tried to give Willow her bottle, only for her to throw up the whole thing over herself, him and the donated sofa. Then she proceeded to have the sort of nappy explosion that he had never imagined outside horror movies. One that he proved inadequate to cleaning up with the usual array of wipes and cloths.

'This wasn't in any of the books,' he muttered to her. 'I'd definitely have noticed illustrations of *this*.'

Willow responded by screwing up her face in a sort of warning way. Eyes wide, Max grabbed for another nappy—but was too late.

Which was why he was standing in the bathroom in nothing but his boxer shorts, trying to clean them both off with tepid water, when Lena found them.

'Don't come in here,' Max told her as he heard

her approach. 'Not unless you're wearing a hazmat suit, anyway.'

She giggled, and Max turned to look at her—finding her leaning in the doorway wearing a beautiful beaded dress of coral-red, her hair pinned up except for one tendril that curled down across her bare neck.

He swallowed. Hard. 'Definitely don't come in here in that. I have no idea how you'd even begin to clean it if Willow soiled it.'

'Carefully,' Lena said. 'And by hand. Are you all right in there? I can go change and take over, if you need.'

Max shook his head. 'Willow and I have just been reaching an understanding by which she never does this to me again. But otherwise, we're almost clean. I'll get her dressed in something not covered in sick or poo, and *then* you can take her, while I take a shower.'

'Sounds like a plan.'

By the time he'd showered long enough to actually feel clean, and dressed in a charcoal suit he hoped matched Lena's levels of dressiness, Hillary Jenkins and Margery had already arrived. He jogged down the stairs to find them cooing over an angelic-looking Willow, in a pristine white sleep suit.

'She's just a little doll, isn't she?' Margery said.

Max didn't comment.

After Lena had left the two women comprehensive instructions, both their mobile numbers *and* the phone number of the restaurant that they themselves had booked, it was too late for them to walk into the village. Not to mention that Max wasn't sure Lena *could* walk that far in the tall, strappy shoes she was wearing. Even if they did do amazing things to her legs…

Max pushed the thought away and concentrated on driving. Lena hadn't given any indication that she considered this a date, and until she did he had to assume this was just a dinner between old friends. Or sleep-deprived pseudo-parents. One of those.

'Well, we made it,' Lena said as they settled into their table at Roberto's.

'I wasn't sure we would, for a while there,' Max admitted.

'Neither was I.' She raised the glass of champagne that Roberto himself had poured for her on arrival, and he picked up his to clink against it. 'Here's to escaping for a night.'

'To escape,' Max echoed.

Except escaping always made him think of *that* night. Of those unexpected hours spent in the back seat of his car with Lena, before he drove out of her life for ever.

Or so he'd thought.

Now he was back, what was it he wanted to escape?

He sipped his champagne anyway—just one glass, since he had to drive them home again, and the last thing he wanted was a hangover when Willow started wailing in the middle of the night.

The restaurant was much as he had expected—checked tablecloths, candles shoved into bottles, and intimate tables for two dotted around the low-beamed room of one of the older buildings on the high street. But the menu surprised him. Max had eaten Italian in some of London's best restaurants, not to mention Rome's, but this menu rivalled them all.

He studied it carefully as he dipped some truly delicious bread into olive oil and balsamic vinegar, then popped it in his mouth.

'I wouldn't bother looking at that too hard,' Lena said, sounding amused. 'Roberto will just bring us out whatever he thinks we'll enjoy anyway.'

'Does anybody in this village let you actually order or do what you want, or do they all think they know what's best for you?' Max asked.

Lena dropped her gaze to the table, a small smile on her lips. 'I guess they all know me pretty well by now, and they like to surprise me. That's all.'

'Or we all know she's such a control freak in her everyday life that it does her good to give it up sometimes,' their waitress said, placing five small bowls on the table.

'That makes more sense,' Max admitted. 'Now, what do we have here?'

What they had, it turned out, was a sort of Italian tapas: five different sorts of pasta in five different sauces, to share. 'Roberto is deciding on your mains now,' the waitress said. 'But get started on these.'

'You first,' Max said to Lena as the waitress backed away.

Lena already had her fork in her hand. 'Mmm, you have to try this walnut one. It's delicious.'

She wasn't wrong. Each of the dishes seemed more delicious than the last—but Max's favourite thing about them was the look of pleasure on Lena's face as she tasted each of them in turn.

I want to make her look like that.

The thought came from nowhere, but Max knew it wouldn't be leaving his brain any time soon.

Last time, their only time, they'd both been young and inexperienced, but enthusiasm had made up for a lot. This time around...if there was a 'this time'...Max knew he could do a whole lot better. After all, not *all* of the past sixteen years had been as much of a drought as the last one. He'd learned things.

Like patience. And timing. And paying attention.

This time, Max knew he could do it right.

And he wouldn't want to escape afterwards, either.

Max was watching her across the table as if she were the most delicious thing on the menu they hadn't been allowed to order from.

Between them the candles flickered, and Lena felt a thrill of something almost forgotten shiver through her. He wanted her. She was sure of it—as sure as she'd been that night in the party. The two of them were unfinished business, in a way. Would tonight be the night they finally finished it?

Max pushed away his empty dessert bowl, just in time for Kelly, their waitress, to swipe it away and replace it with a large cup of coffee. Then she placed a mint tea in front of Lena, with a shrug. 'Roberto says it's better for helping you sleep.'

'Roberto doesn't think I need sleep?' Max asked, once Kelly had returned to the kitchen.

'Hard to say,' Lena admitted. Roberto was generally a law unto himself anyway. 'It's always possible he's given you decaf.'

Huffing a laugh, Max reached for his coffee cup. 'I think today, more than anything since I arrived, has definitely proved that Wells-on-Water has changed from the village I remember.'

'I'm glad you think so.' She felt a strange warmth at his admission. Almost as if she had fixed this place that had driven him away, which wasn't at all true.

Firstly, she could hardly claim responsibility for Roberto's family moving to the village and setting up a restaurant, or a hundred other changes.

Secondly, she still didn't know for sure if he'd be staying, once everything was settled with Willow. He still had next to no furniture in his house, and a life in London she couldn't imagine he was in a hurry to leave behind.

Still. She liked knowing that he'd recognised how Wells-on-Water had changed—for the better.

'The way people have treated Willow, and talked about her mother, despite everything…it says a lot,' Max went on. 'It makes me wonder what it would be like for me, and for my mum, if I'd grown up here now.'

'Different, I hope.' Lena met his gaze across the table and smiled. 'Mind you, you probably would still have got into trouble with Hillary Jenkins regularly, even now.'

Max laughed. 'Probably. God, if I could tell my twelve-year-old self that one day Mrs Jenkins from the corner shop would be offering to babysit for me so I could go out for dinner with Lena Phillips.' He shook his head. 'I'd never believe it. Especially the part about it being with you.'

Lena was pretty sure the heat that hit her cheeks at his words wasn't entirely due to the peppermint tea or the candlelight. Much more likely it had to do with the warmth in his eyes as he held her gaze, the slow smile that made her heartbeat kick up a notch. The reminder that this man had been the first to ever see her naked—and she wanted him to again.

Clearing her throat, she broke away from his gaze and cast about for a safer topic of conversation. One that definitely wouldn't lead to her trying to seduce him on top of Roberto's best table.

'Do you remember that bonfire night?' she asked, apropos of nothing, but Max seemed to know immediately what she was talking about.

'With the Catherine wheel that broke free from the fence and chased Mrs Jenkins around the village green?' He laughed, the sound ringing genuinely around the restaurant. 'Who could forget? I swear, at that moment, that was the best night of my life.'

'Others have surpassed it since, I imagine?'

Oh, but she wasn't imagining the fire in his eyes. 'One or two.'

She looked away. Again.

Would it always be like this? Leading him to the edge of a conversation about the two of them, about what it meant that they were there together, then losing her nerve? Probably, she admitted to herself. She was great at getting others to do what was needed, it seemed, but when it came to convincing herself to take action… well. There, she was a failure.

And it wasn't as if there weren't complicating factors between them. Willow, his life in London…and other things she wasn't ready to face yet, either.

Max seemed to recognise her need to change the subject.

'So, what happened to the pub?' he asked.

'Which pub?' Lena felt her brow furrow. 'The King's Arms in Wishcliffe?'

'No, The Fox. Your family pub.'

As if she could forget the pub her family had owned and run her entire life.

'Nothing happened to it,' she told him, baffled by the question. 'It's right where you left it.'

'But…your family don't own it any longer?' He sounded as confused as she felt. 'Victoria said you were managing the King's Arms instead.'

Oh. *Now* she understood.

Lena looked down at her mint tea, swirling the real mint leaves around with the silver teaspoon. ‘No, we still own it. The boys run it, since Dad died.’

Max leaned back in his chair and gave her that look she was beginning to recognise all too well. The one that meant he was about to call her out on some aspect of her life, and Lena decided she’d rather not hear it right now, so she spoke again first.

‘I went away to uni, you know, after you left. I’d planned to stay close by, so I could live at home and commute in for lectures.’ She chose her words carefully, picking her way between the things she was willing to tell, and the secrets she still wanted to keep.

‘I remember,’ Max said softly, not interrupting, just confirming that he was paying attention.

‘But after…well, after that night, with you. When you talked about getting out and seeing the world…I guess I wanted a slice of that, too. I always knew I’d end up back here—Wells-on-Water is just where I belong. But I decided that didn’t mean I couldn’t see a bit of the world outside first. So I went through clearing and got a place at a university up in the north, to study hospitality and marketing.’ All true. Just not the whole truth.

Lies of omission are still lies, Lena...

'What did your father and brothers think about that?' That one question told her that he really *did* remember everything she'd said that night. About how she was tied to home, and family, and the pub, since her mother's death. That they needed her.

'They...weren't pleased.' Understatement of the century. 'I tried to convince them that me studying these things would help us build up business at the pub, but they weren't buying it. There was a bit of a scene.' She hadn't told them the truth, either, about why she'd needed to leave. Her father would never have understood, and her brothers...

Well. She knew full well what they thought.

'I can imagine. But you went anyway.' His smile looked almost proud. He wouldn't smile like that if he knew the truth, she was sure.

He probably thought this was all because of him. Which, well, maybe it was, but she wasn't going to let him be smug about it.

'I am capable of making my own decisions,' she said. And she had, until that had been taken away from her, too.

'I never, for a single moment, doubted that.'

Her heart felt too tight at all the memories she'd tried so hard to forget. She pushed on, eager to reach the end of this story. 'Anyway, I studied and I learned and I came home in the holidays and worked in the pub like always, and then when I graduated…nothing changed.'

'How do you mean?' Max asked.

'I had all these ideas and dreams for The Fox—I mean, it was my home, and I remembered how it used to be when Mum was alive. Full of families and good food, a real social hub of the community. But after she was gone… well, you know.'

'It went downhill,' Max said, which Lena thought was generous.

'The majority of people who went there were old men who were already too drunk to care about the sticky floor and the truly grim bathrooms,' she said. 'I did my best, but the changes it needed were huge, and they wouldn't let me make any of them.'

'So you left.'

'Not immediately.' Lena gave a small half-shrug. 'But eventually I got sick of drunk old men trying to feel me up. I applied for a job at the King's Arms instead and got it. The manager there liked my ideas, and actually implemented a lot of them. The pub got more popular as word got around and, well, when the manager left they promoted me to his job.'

'And the place went from strength to strength, from what I've heard.' Max smiled at her. 'Although, I have to admit, it was a bit of a shock to see Wishcliffe featured in a "Britain's Best Hidden Pubs" feature in a London paper last month. If it had said that you were behind it, maybe I wouldn't have been so surprised.'

That feature had been the pinnacle of her career so far; she couldn't quite believe he'd actually read it. And suddenly she didn't mind so much if Max felt a bit responsible for her achievements. Because, in a way, he was.

Before she could stop herself, she met his gaze across the table, and told him the truth. Maybe not all of it, but enough, for now.

'You were my first rebellion, you know. Without you...I don't know if I'd have done any of it.'

CHAPTER NINE

MAX BLINKED, her words echoing in his head but still making no sense.

'I don't think I can take any credit for that,' he said. 'Everything you've done, you've done it yourself, Lena.'

She smiled. 'Yes, I have. But it's true. That night with you… You know, my whole life until then I'd done the Right Thing. What people expected from me. I didn't cause trouble—because I knew that wouldn't be fair to my dad with my mum gone, and three kids and a pub to look after. I did all the right things in school, partly to try and make up for the hell my brothers had put all the teachers through before me. I was polite to everyone, helped everyone, dressed in a way even Mrs Jenkins couldn't object to…because this village had saved us, after Mum died. They'd looked after Dad, even the people who didn't like him or his pub. They'd even given the boys more chances than they deserved. And they took care of me, a poor, motherless girl. All because they'd all loved Mum.'

'From what I remember, she was a very loveable woman,' Max said. 'I never heard anyone say a bad word against her. Much like you.' He didn't tell her how many people had stopped him over the past day or so, when they were out and about or when people brought things to the house, to tell him to look after Lena. To protect her.

She mattered to everyone in the village, because she'd given everything she had to them.

He hadn't known how to tell them how much she mattered to him, too.

And he *really* hated to think how fast they'd kick him back out of Wells-on-Water if they ever learned that he'd taken teenage Lena's virginity and then run out on her.

'The point is, I never thought about what *I* wanted. I only considered what was the right thing to do. Until that night with you.'

Max barked a laugh at that. 'Because I was definitely *not* the right thing to do.'

The smile that spread across Lena's face at that warmed something deep inside him. 'Oh, I don't know. There are definitely worse choices for a girl's first time,' she said. 'But, no. I don't think anyone in the village would have approved of me seducing you in the back seat of your car on the last day of sixth form.'

'And here I was thinking that I seduced you.'

The look she gave him completely dispelled that idea.

'But I wanted you, just for myself,' Lena went on quietly. 'That night, the way we talked, the things I learned about you… I'd lived side by side with you my whole life, and never seen inside your heart and soul that way before. Never really known you. And when I did…'

'I left,' Max reminded her bluntly. Right now, it was hard to remember why, or even how, he'd walked away from her. Except leaving Wells-on-Water had been his ambition for so much of his life, perhaps it was always going to take more than one night to overturn it.

But she hadn't been the only one who felt as if they'd got to know a whole new person that night.

'You did,' Lena allowed. 'But before you went, you showed me it was okay to want things beyond the village. To want something just for me, not for anyone else. Like I say, you were my first rebellion. The ones that came after were all the easier because I'd already done it before.'

He wasn't sure what to say to that. On the one hand, it didn't seem to him that Lena had lived a particularly rebellious life. But by her own standards, she had. She'd left home. She'd found another job when her family wouldn't let her grow where she was. She had turned Wells-on-Water into the kind of community she always knew it could be, but that it wasn't always—not to him, for starters—without her influence.

Max thought that maybe more rebellions should be like Lena's. Quiet, determined—and world-changing, for the people living in that world.

'If I have played any small part in helping you become the woman you are today, then I'm proud of that,' he said. 'And just grateful to have been there.'

He held her gaze for a long moment, watching her cheeks turn pink in the candlelight, and hoping she felt the truth in every word.

'We should get back to Willow,' she said, after a long moment.

'And Mrs Jenkins,' Max agreed. 'Who knows what she'll have done to my house in my absence otherwise?'

'You know that she's going to have gone through all your drawers, right?' Lena teased.

Max nodded. 'That's why I hid the really scandalous stuff in your room.'

Roberto wouldn't accept payment for the meal, but Max managed to slip a couple of notes into the tip jar for Kelly, the waitress, at least.

They drove home in silence and found the lights of the Manor House still blazing against the fallen twilight on their arrival. It looked almost welcoming, lit up like that, Max thought, staring up at it as he exited the car.

'What?' Lena asked as he paused. 'What's the matter?'

'Nothing. I just…it's always dark when I arrive,' he explained. 'I've never seen it like this before. It looks…'

'Like a home?' she finished for him.

'Yeah,' Max breathed. 'I guess it does.'

But he knew in his heart it wasn't just a few lamps that made it feel that way. And he had a terrible feeling that Lena's ongoing rebellion might have stretched as far as his house, too.

Worse still, it might have infected his heart.

Hillary and Margery were pleased that they'd had a good time and swore that Willow hadn't been a bother at all, but the speed at which they left suggested they might have been stretching the truth a little on that point.

Still, she'd had a bottle recently, and was contentedly sleeping in her Moses basket, so Max carried her carefully up the stairs, as Lena ran ahead to open doors and clear the way.

'Want me to take first shift tonight?' she asked as they reached the hallway.

Max shook his head, then winced as the basket shook, too. 'You sleep. You've been up for hours, and I'm better at late nights, anyway.'

'If you're sure.' As tired as she was, there was a part of Lena that just didn't want the night to end. Not yet.

Something still felt…unfinished.

'Just wait here a second.' Max disappeared into his bedroom, and through the open door she watched him place the basket carefully on the stand someone had donated, peering in at Willow and straightening her blankets.

He was good with her, in a way Lena really hadn't expected. If he hadn't been so certain that she *couldn't* be his, she'd have suspected some sort of paternal instinct.

Finally satisfied with the blanket arrangement, he re-emerged, pulling the door almost closed behind him, but open enough that they'd still hear Willow easily if she woke.

'Everything okay?' Lena whispered.

'She's fine,' Max replied. 'I just wanted to…'

She thought he'd stumble for the right words. Maybe try to thank her for staying and helping with the baby, or something.

Instead, he leaned in and cupped a hand against the back of her neck.

'I've wanted to kiss you all night,' he murmured, so close she could feel the words against her skin. 'May I?'

All the reasons she'd been telling herself why this was a bad idea flew from her head. Swallowing, she nodded, and tilted her lips up to meet his.

She'd thought she remembered his kiss well. Thought she remembered everything about the night they'd spent together.

But this kiss was nothing like their teenage fumblings, so either she was remembering wrong, or Max had learned a *lot* in the intervening years.

He teased her mouth open with his tongue, his lips always moving over hers, caressing and warming her mouth, sending shots of sheer lust shooting through her body. Apart from his hand at her neck they weren't touching at all, Max keeping just enough distance between them that, if she wanted it closed, it would have to be her choice.

And, oh, she *did* want to close that gap. But given how Max was setting her whole body on fire with just a kiss, she wasn't sure she could risk it.

'Lena...' He breathed her name against her mouth. 'God, Lena.'

'I know,' she whispered back. 'I know.'

Exactly what she knew, she wasn't sure. But whatever it was he was right there with her.

Maybe this was one of those times where she just had to throw caution to the wind. Forget the past, forget tomorrow, and just enjoy the now.

Closing her eyes, she shifted her whole body towards him, sinking into his kiss as she brought her hands up to press against his back and keep him close. Max made a sound somewhere in the back of his throat that didn't even sound like a word, and deepened the kiss beyond the mind-bending experience it already was.

God, she could feel him hard against her, pressing into her stomach, showing her exactly how much he wanted her. And she remembered that, too. How desperate he'd been to touch her, to kiss her, to be inside her…

But in other ways this was *nothing* like their first time together. They were grown-ups now. There was no taboo here, no rebellion—no real reason at all she couldn't spend the night with this single, devastatingly attractive man if she wanted, without having to believe it would lead anywhere. He could leave again tomorrow and it wouldn't break her heart, or her spirit, just as it hadn't last time.

Max's hands had wandered to her back now, one roaming down to cup her backside and hold her against him, the other splayed across her spine. She felt a sudden jolt against her back and realised he'd spun them—away from the risk of the stairs, so her back was against the wall between their two bedroom doors.

Another reason it could be so much better than their first time: they had access to an actual bed this time.

'Max,' she said, the word swallowed into his desperate kisses. 'We should—'

He stopped, pulling back just enough to meet her gaze, and she could see his chest heaving with the effort. 'Stop?' There was actual pain in the word, she could hear it.

She smiled. 'Find a bed.'

'Oh, thank God.' He kissed her again, then grabbed her hand. 'Your room?'

She hesitated, just for a moment. 'We'll still hear Willow?'

As if in answer, a cry went up from inside Max's room, a thin, little wail that spoke of hunger, or the need for a cuddle or a dry nappy.

Max's forehead hit the wall beside her head. 'Apparently so.'

'I'll go.' She began to wiggle her way out of his arms, but Max shook his head.

'No. It's my turn. You go get some rest.'

'You'll find me after?' She wasn't ready to give up this moment, this opportunity, just yet.

Max gave her a small smile. 'I most definitely will.'

Willow cried out again, and Max pushed away

from the wall, turning to head into his room. Lena watched him go, admiring the way his shirt stretched across his back—who even knew what had happened to his jacket?—and the perfect fit of his trousers…

She shook her head, as all those reasons she'd forgotten came rushing back. Willow was what mattered most right now. Max was right; she needed to go rest.

After all, if she and Max ever got the chance to follow through on what they'd started tonight, she was going to need all her energy.

Two hours later, Max was starting to wonder if Willow had a personal objection to her two current carers finding any sort of pleasure or happiness in each other's arms, or if it was just a coincidence that nothing in the world seemed to settle her tonight.

He'd tried changing her, feeding her, winding her, rocking her, re-wrapping her blankets in the special way Janice had taught them… everything. In the end, he resorted to pacing around the house with Willow in his arms, humming low in his chest the way she seemed to like. It stopped the screaming—at least, as long as he didn't try to put her down.

Eventually, though, even Willow's tenacious desire to stay awake gave way and, not long before the sun started rising, she finally fell properly asleep again. Gingerly, Max laid her back in her Moses basket, and considered what to do next.

Lena had to be asleep by now. And as much as he wanted to go and wake her, he knew he was on the edge of exhaustion, too. Even if they were both able to stay awake long enough to make love, he didn't kid himself for a second that he'd be able to perform at his best.

Surely it must be better to both get some sleep, and hope they got a better opportunity later.

It was just that he'd never been a very patient man.

And what if she *wasn't* asleep? What if she was lying awake and waiting for him? He at least owed it to her to check, right?

But when he peered around her bedroom door, the room was in darkness, and he could just make out the gentle rise and fall of the duvet wrapped around her as Lena breathed the slow, regular breaths of a deep sleep.

No, he couldn't wake her up. He'd just have to hope that she was still willing to revisit this development of their relationship again tomorrow.

Max padded back to his bedroom, checked on Willow one last time, then slipped gratefully between the sheets on his bed and let his body relax.

For now, he'd just rest up in readiness.

Willow was gone from her basket when Max awoke the next morning, but he could hear Lena singing sweetly to her downstairs, so he allowed himself a moment to wake up properly and take a shower before heading down to join them.

By the time he got there, though, the singing had ended and Lena was frowning at her phone, while Willow bounced in her fabric chair on the floor.

'Everything okay?' He dropped a kiss onto Willow's forehead, then moved towards the coffee machine. God bless whoever had upgraded theirs and donated this one to the Manor House; Max really wasn't sure he'd have made it through this week so far without it.

'Hmm,' Lena replied, which told him nothing.

Max checked her coffee mug and, finding it empty, refilled it for her. Maybe that would help.

'Thanks.' She gave him a tight smile as she took it from him.

Rocking back on his heels as he waited for his own coffee to brew, he watched as her attention returned to her phone. 'Everything okay?' he asked again.

'Just a message from work. They've been great about me having time off to help with Willow this week, but I think I'm going to have to go in today. I can probably take Willow with me…'

But she wouldn't be able to concentrate on whatever had her frowning like that, Max was sure.

'Leave her here,' Max said. 'I've got to do some work today, too, but I reckon she'll be a dab hand at filing in no time.' He'd managed a full hour alone with her yesterday. And yes, it had ended with them both covered in bodily waste and in desperate need of a shower, but nothing really terrible had happened. A little longer alone with her today couldn't be any worse, right?

'Are you sure?' Lena worried her bottom lip with her teeth. 'If you got video calls or meetings…'

'She'll be fine,' Max assured her. 'Besides, I'm the boss. If she acts up, they'll just have to deal with it.'

'If you're absolutely certain…'

'I am.' He wasn't, not really, but he could tell from Lena's nervous tapping of her coffee cup, the way she was still biting down on her lip, that whatever was going on at work was important, and she needed to focus on it.

This might not be the conversation he'd *wanted* to be having with her this morning, but there was no point trying to discuss what had almost happened between them the night before while she was worried about work stuff.

Lena nodded, decision made. 'Okay, then. I mean, you know where everything is, it's your house, and you've spent as much time looking after Willow as I have, so I guess I'll…go.'

'I'll see you later,' he said, with a warm smile. 'In fact, I'll even root around in the freezer, see what delicious delights the neighbours have left us for dinner.'

'Perfect little house husband, huh?' Lena joked, then her eyes widened. 'Not that I'm saying… I mean, I'm not assuming…last night…'

'Lena,' he interrupted. 'I have just enough social skills to understand when something is a joke, rumours notwithstanding. Go sort out whatever it is you need to sort out, and we'll talk later. Okay?'

'Later. Right.' With a swift smile, Lena downed the rest of her coffee, then moved from the table to kneel on the stone floor beside Willow to kiss her goodbye. 'You be good for Max today, you hear?'

'Oh, we'll get along famously, I'm sure.' Max was under no illusions after the past few days; he fully expected his day to be interrupted by cries for milk and hideous nappies. But, to his immense surprise, he found that he was okay with that.

Lena stood up and, after a moment of obvious deliberation, bent to press a quick kiss to Max's lips, too. 'Later,' she said, and Max heard it for what it was.

A promise.

The hardest part, Max found, was trying to type, or hold a phone, with Willow in his arms. While she'd be happy in the Chair of Joy for short periods—he really must stop calling it that—inevitably she wanted to be held or fed or changed just when he needed to do something that required both arms.

He was wrestling with a spreadsheet with one hand, while rocking Willow in the other arm, when Toby called.

'So, this talking on the phone thing is something we do now?' Max asked, in lieu of a greeting.

'Apparently,' Toby replied, nonplussed. 'I just thought I'd check in and see how things are going. I understand from Autumn, who had it from Victoria, who heard it from God knows who in the village, that Willow is still with you?'

'She is.'

'And that you even had Hillary Jenkins babysitting for you last night.' The awe in Toby's voice suggested to Max that his half-brother's history with the formidable Mrs Jenkins might not be miles away from his own, albeit for different reasons.

'I think that was probably for Lena's benefit.'

'Ah. That makes sense,' Toby said. 'So, how *is* it going?'

I can't decide which is distracting me from work most: the baby, or thinking about Lena and last night...

'I'm trying to type up some figures while also persuading Willow to go to sleep. Basically, I need an extra arm. Maybe two.' Octopuses had the right idea, he decided, when it came to juggling childcare and work.

Toby laughed. 'Lena isn't there?'

'She had to go into work.' And that was distracting him, too. She'd looked worried this morning—not just 'someone screwed up the order of scallops' worried, or 'someone called in sick' worried. Genuinely concerned about something that mattered.

He wondered if she'd tell him what it was, later.

If he survived until later without his arm falling off.

Holding the phone between his ear and shoulder, he switched Willow to his other arm.

'Have you got one of those sling things?' Toby asked vaguely.

'I have literally no idea what you're talking about,' Max replied.

'Autumn brought one home from her baby shower. Actually, she brought two, for some ungodly reason, and insisted on demonstrating both of them with some doll that someone had given her. They're for holding the baby against your chest, so they feel like they're being held but you can actually get on with doing things. Apparently babies love it.'

A sling. Part of his brain rebelled against the idea of being some sort of yummy daddy with a baby strapped to his chest. But another, larger part countered that this was a way that both arms could be his own again *and* he could still hold Willow to stop her crying. It didn't have to mean anything about his personality, or that this situation was going to go on much longer.

Practicality won out. 'Do you think Autumn would mind if I borrowed one?'

CHAPTER TEN

LENA CUT THE ENGINE, parked her little yellow car neatly outside the Manor House, but made no move to get out. She needed just a moment to process the day before she re-entered the cosy world she'd created with Max and Willow. Before she tried to have that *later* conversation that Max had put off that morning.

Why was it that, whenever something was finally going well in the world, something else had to get screwed up to balance it out?

The late-afternoon air was still warm with summer sun, and she had the window open to let in a breeze. Outside, she could hear the contented buzz of insects, the drone of a plane overhead—probably a vintage one from the local airfield, by the sound of it—and the wind as it rustled the leaves of the trees that edged the property.

And above it all, she could hear Max. Yelling.

She frowned. No, not quite *yelling*, but certainly talking forcefully at somebody.

Unbuckling her seat belt, she climbed out of the car and headed around the side of the Manor House, towards the sound.

As she turned the corner onto the back lawn, she spotted him, pacing away towards the trees at the far end, one hand holding his mobile phone to his ear, the other gesticulating wildly. Clearly this was a work call, from the snatches of words that reached her on the breeze—*targets, projections, stakeholders...*

So where was Willow? Panicked, Lena glanced around the terrace at the back of the house, looking for the Chair of Joy, but there was no sign. And the back doors were closed, and Max wouldn't have shut her in the house on her own, Lena was sure of it.

Then Max turned to begin pacing back towards the Manor House, and Lena noticed the baby sling strapped to his chest, her breath whooshing out of her chest in relief.

Spotting her, Max ended his call and shoved his phone into his pocket, picking up his pace to almost a jog as he headed towards her. 'You're back.'

'I am,' she said, with a smile she didn't quite feel. 'And I see you've found a new way to manage babysitting and working at the same time.'

'It was Toby's idea,' Max admitted, looking mildly uncomfortable at being caught in such a domesticated set-up. 'Autumn had two, so he brought one over and, countless YouTube tutorials later, here we are.'

'It's a good idea. So, your day has been okay?' She should be grateful that at least one of them had had a good day, she supposed. Even if it wasn't her.

'It's been fine.' Max frowned. Possibly her smile wasn't as convincing as she'd hoped. 'What went wrong with yours?'

Lena sighed. 'Basically? Everything.'

He put an arm around her shoulder and guided her towards the door. 'Come on. If you promise not to laugh at me for going full-on stay-at-home dad, there's some sort of chicken casserole thing in the oven, and a bottle of wine chilling in the fridge for you.'

'If those are the conditions, I think I can manage.' It wouldn't do to tell him how adorable she found his descent into domesticity.

'Good. Then I'll get Willow out of this thing, pour you a glass of wine, and you can tell me all about it.'

Lena let herself be led, and tried not to think about how easy it would be to get used to all of this.

'So, they're selling the King's Arms,' Max said some time later, when Willow was back in her Chair of Joy, full of milk and ready to sleep, and the two of them were sitting at the kitchen table sharing out someone's family recipe for chicken casserole. 'Why?'

Lena shrugged, and snagged another potato from the pot. 'Because they can, I guess. There's a buzz around the place and a good offer came in, from some celebrity chef who wants to build on what we've already done with the place.'

'And will they keep you on as manager?' Max topped up her glass, and she realised she'd already drunk half of it. She'd have to slow down, or getting up at four in the morning with Willow would be unbearable.

'They might.' Harold, the current owner, hadn't been completely clear on that point. 'Or they might have their own people they want to bring in. And even if they do want me to stay…'

'You're not sure if you want to,' Max guessed, and Lena nodded. It was nice to have someone to talk this through with, she realised. Someone who understood, if not the specifics, at least the feeling she had about her career, and wanting to take charge of it.

'Part of the fun of working there for me has always been the freedom to do things my own way. And I can already tell from everything Harold has said that wouldn't be the case with the new owners.'

'Maybe it's time to start looking for a new challenge, then?' Max suggested.

'Perhaps.' Lena sighed. 'But there's only so many pubs in this neck of the woods left that haven't been turned into houses. And of them, there aren't many that would be suitable, and I don't know that any of them would take me.' Especially not her brothers, still running The Fox into the ground in the village.

'They'd all be lucky to have you.' Max reached across the table and took her hand in his. 'But there are other things you could do—other challenges you could turn your many talents to.'

'Maybe.' It was just hard to see forward to any of them, when she was still mourning the hard work she'd put in that would now be lost. Not just the King's Arms, but the community hub as well.

Perhaps the universe was trying to send her a message. Time to move on with her life.

Except Wells-on-Water *was* her life, it always had been. And she wasn't sure she was ready to give any of it up without a fight.

She looked up at Max and wondered, just for a flicker of a second, what it would be like to seek that next step on her ladder in London, with him. Then she shook the thought away again.

This week, here at the Manor House with him

and Willow, was a moment out of time, that was all. As the night they'd lost their virginities together had been. It wasn't what real life, or a real relationship between them, would be like.

She couldn't afford to let herself get swept up in that fairy tale. Not when she was already worrying about how bruised her heart might be when this moment ended.

Not when the memories of the aftermath last time still haunted her.

Max supposed he should be grateful that Willow had managed to stay peaceful and content while Lena had told him about everything that was happening at the King's Arms. But the fact she started wailing the moment dinner was over, and didn't stop for well over an hour and a half, wore away a lot of that gratitude. Eventually, once she'd taken her bottle, he put her back in the sling and paced around the garden in the cooling night air, where she acted like his own little hot-water bottle.

He'd sent Lena upstairs for a bath, and an early night, sensing that, with everything that had gone on today, this wasn't the *later* they were waiting for to continue last night's… conversation. But that didn't stop him wondering what she might have said, if they *had* had the opportunity.

Or imagining a different universe where he might join her in that bath, instead of pacing up and down with a fractious baby.

Thinking about Lena was a bad road to head down, especially alone in the night—well, alone except for a dozing Willow pressed against his chest.

Maybe it was just as well that Willow had interrupted them the night before, because Max really wasn't sure where they'd have been heading. Except for bed, that much seemed clear. But what then?

He sighed, and looked down at the downy hair on Willow's head, pressing a kiss against it as his thoughts swirled.

Sixteen years ago, he'd seduced Lena—or she'd seduced him, depending on who you asked—and run out on her hours later. He'd left her without a backward thought. Well, not many, anyway. And never enough to make him turn around and return to Wells-on-Water.

Since then, they'd both forged their own lives—and it was only a coincidence that had brought them back together again.

If Victoria hadn't reintroduced them at the party. If Lena's idiot brothers hadn't knocked dessert all over the floor. If he hadn't stained his shirt. If the village taxis ran past nine o'clock. If not for all those things, Lena would never have been with him when he'd found Willow on his doorstep.

He'd have handed the baby over to the proper authorities, and gone about his life again, whatever that damned note said. He'd have stayed holed up at the Manor House until it was set up, then headed back to London and work, as had been his plan. He'd have used the house for the odd party, or a getaway, or to visit Toby and Autumn, occasionally, but that was all. And his path might never have crossed Lena Phillips's again.

It had been the same sixteen years ago, he remembered suddenly.

If he hadn't had a fight with his mum and walked out, he never would have joined the usual crowd of cooler kids hanging out down by the river. If she hadn't had a fight with her brothers that evening, she wouldn't have been feeling so edgy and out of sorts that she'd drifted away from her friends towards him. If he hadn't been for a drive to check the car was running okay before he left for London the next day, he'd have walked, and they'd have had nowhere to go. If her friends hadn't been stupid and drunk, they'd have noticed she was missing sooner. If they hadn't both been feeling so out of place that night, they never would have started talking.

And if they hadn't talked that night—really talked, for the first time ever, even after years of growing up in the same village, being in the same class, and knowing all the same people—they definitely would not have ended up naked in the back of his car, parked up behind some of the abandoned sheds on the edge of the Wishcliffe estate.

The talking, he thought, had surprised him even more than the sex. To discover there was so much more to Lena Phillips—so much under that surface of good girl, popular girl, nice girl, and every other label people gave her. Or perhaps she gave herself.

And now, here at the Manor House with Willow, it was the talking that had undone him again.

Last night, hearing her talk about her rebellions, had been one such moment. But it was so much more than that. Chatting with her over coffee, discussing Willow's little ways. Watching her talk to the people of the village. Hearing her speak about the community hub she'd worked so hard for, and lost through no fault of her own. How much she'd given to the King's Arms only to have it snatched away.

Every moment he spent with Lena seemed to drag him deeper.

Had he known this would happen, sixteen

years ago? Was that why he'd run so far and so fast after their night together?

No.

He'd run because he was eighteen and stupid and hadn't even realised what was in front of him.

What worried him now was that he wasn't sure he wouldn't run again.

He stopped at the edge of the trees and turned to look back at the shadow of the Manor House against the night sky. He'd left one small light burning in the kitchen, but the rest of the house was in darkness. Abandoned. If he didn't know Lena was sleeping inside, he'd assume he and Willow were alone.

Soon, Willow would go—back to her mother or family, if they could find them, or to social services if not. Because, as much as he might have not hated playing house with Lena, it wasn't real. It wasn't even *right*, by anyone's standards. He could hear his mother nagging about doing the right thing, even now, across years and years and the divide of death.

The right thing would be to admit that Willow *couldn't* be his daughter, and let her find a real home. One with loving parents who knew what they were doing, and didn't take two hours of YouTube videos to figure out how to use a sling. With a loving couple who adored each other, as well as Willow, perhaps, rather than two people wanting to recreate a one-night stand. Or at least a single parent who was ready to fight and strive for their child the way his own mother had.

The right thing would be to set Lena free to find her own future again, wherever that might be.

Max wasn't under any illusions that whatever had caught fire between them last night would last, any more than it had sixteen years ago. Lena had only stayed at all because of Willow, and once she was gone, Lena would be, too.

Lena was a good person. A loving, honest, kind person. And Max had never been any of those things.

He was a troublemaker. A grumpy, single-minded, oblivious fool, according to more than one of his ex-girlfriends. He wasn't good at relationships, or people, and if Lena truly believed that the people of Wells-on-Water might change their mind about him after all these years…well, she always had been an incurable optimist.

He knew that he'd only been tolerated here this week because of Lena, and because he was helping Willow—even if the locals did believe he might be responsible for fathering her. Once this was over, they'd all remember why they despised him again.

And then it would be time for him to leave, whatever Toby said.

Whatever he was starting to think he might want.

The next day went more smoothly than the day before had, in some ways. Lena woke late, but found Willow and Max both asleep in his room. Their *later* conversation still hadn't occurred, but she had hope that it might today. Now she was over the initial shock of yesterday's news, she felt almost ready to face the future. Especially if it had more of Max's kisses in it.

When Willow stirred, Lena took her downstairs and started their day together with a clean nappy and milk for the baby, and coffee for her.

A little while later, she was surprised by a knock on the door—and even more surprised to find Kathy and Trevor on the doorstep when she answered it.

'We thought you might like some company,' Kathy said, eyeing the bundle of baby in Lena's arms. 'You know, of the not-infant variety.'

'Thought we could take a walk down to the cafe or something,' Trevor added. 'We'd offer to take the baby for you but—'

'We really wouldn't know what to do with one,' Kathy admitted. 'So you'd probably better come, too.'

Lena beamed at her friends. 'That would lovely. Hang on.'

Letting Kathy and Trevor inside, she popped Willow in the Chair of Joy and set about getting things together to leave the house—which always took far longer than seemed reasonable.

She'd planned to leave Max a note but, hearing movement from his room—and realising that Willow's best blanket was in there, too—she headed up to tell him herself, leaving a nervous Kathy and Trevor to watch the baby for a moment.

'Max?' Lena pushed open his bedroom door when there was no response, but found the room empty. Frowning, she hunted for the blanket and, having found it, was about to turn and leave when the door to the en-suite bathroom opened. And out stepped Max.

He wasn't naked, at least. Lena was almost certain that was a good thing. But the low-slung towel around his waist left very little to the imagination all the same.

She swallowed, her mouth suddenly very dry, and realised she was staring.

'Lena?' Max paused in rubbing a second towel over his hair. 'Is everything okay?'

Unable to find words just then, Lena nodded, and held up the blanket as evidence.

Max lowered the towel in his hands and

watched her, a slow smile spreading across his face. 'You're sure? You look somewhat… distracted.'

She shook her head. 'I'm fine. Just came to tell you…' Damn it, what had she come to tell him?

'To tell me…?' He took a step closer, and she could feel the warmth radiating from his skin after his shower. He rested a hand at her waist, and she looked up into his eyes to see an even greater heat building there.

God, what if she'd come up here a minute or two earlier? What if she'd stepped into the bathroom and found him, naked in the shower?

What if she'd joined him…?

'Lena? Are you ready?' Trevor's booming voice echoed up the stairs and shook Lena out of her daze.

Without stepping back, she glanced over her shoulder, hoping her friends wouldn't come up to find her. 'Trevor and Kathy are here. We're going to take Willow for a walk down to the cafe and get a coffee.'

'Right.' Max's voice sounded husky, and he cleared his throat before continuing. 'I'll…uh… get some work done this morning, then. So I can take over with her when you get back.'

Lena nodded. 'That would be good. I need to head down to the King's Arms after lunch.'

'Of course.'

But neither of them moved. They just kept staring, letting the crackle of tension and want between them grow.

Maybe they didn't need to have that *later* conversation. Maybe they just needed to jump each other's bones and have done with it. Like last time…

'Lena?' Kathy's voice had joined Trevor's now, and she sounded closer. As if she was climbing the stairs…

'Coming!' Lena yelled. Clearly Trevor and Kathy were getting antsy alone with the baby. 'I'd better…'

'Yeah. Okay.'

Turning, Lena moved towards the door, but paused, one hand on the frame, to look back at him. 'Later, though?'

'Definitely later,' Max said, adjusting his towel.

Lena grinned, and headed downstairs to rescue Trevor and Kathy.

After coffee and cake with her friends, Lena returned to the Manor House with just enough time to hand Willow over to Max so she could spend the afternoon at work at the King's Arms. The atmosphere in the pub was tense and frosty, despite the sun beating down on the beer garden, and full tables all along the riverbank. It was almost enough to dampen Lena's enthusiasm about the evening ahead with Max—but not quite. Every time she felt it slipping, she remembered him in that towel, and smiled.

She rushed back after work, and found Max still on a work call, with Willow asleep in her Chair of Joy. Flashing him a quick smile, she went to pour herself a glass of wine and bung another freezer meal in the oven.

It was done just in time for Max to join her, and they settled at the table together. Lena's pulse kicked up again just at the sight of him, and she hoped that Willow would sleep tonight, for once.

She was so tired of waiting for *later*.

But for now, everything felt perfectly domestic, and happy and easy.

Until Max said, 'Janice called earlier. She wants to stop by with that social worker this evening.'

Lena froze with a mouthful of food halfway between her plate and her lips. 'Did she say what about?'

Max, chewing, shook his head, even as he loaded up another forkful. He swallowed, and said, 'No. But I imagine it's to do with Willow, don't you?'

'Yes, but what about her?' Lena dropped her fork to her plate. Her heart pounded against her ribcage, a reminder that everything could change in just one of those beats, and life would never be the same again.

She'd experienced it the day her mother died, and again when her father passed on. It had been there that night with Max and again when she told her family she was going away for university. And that awful day that September, when her whole world had felt as if it were ending.

She'd felt it when her father's will had left the pub to her brothers, and her only her mother's jewellery. It had happened the day the roof had caved in on the community hub. And she'd felt it as recently as yesterday, as Harold had told her he was selling the King's Arms.

What would it be this time? That they'd found the mother, or another relative? That they were taking her into care? That Max had to take a DNA test they knew would be negative? What?

Lena pushed her plate away, her appetite gone.

'I don't know exactly what Janice is going to tell us,' Max said, watching her cautiously. 'But we both knew that this situation wasn't going to go on for ever.'

Lena stared at him. It was funny. Two days she'd been waiting for their *later* conversation, and now they were there and it was nothing like she'd expected.

'No, of course not,' she said faintly. Because she *had* known that.

She had known, intellectually, that Willow would be leaving soon. That *she* would be leaving. Hell, she'd been the one fighting for more time to find Willow's mum so they could reunite them without Willow being whisked off into care.

But in her heart… Well. Her heart had got used to being here at the Manor House with Max and Willow. It had got used to being needed and having a place. It had got used to late-night conversations with Max and early-morning grunts over coffee. It had got used to the tired way he smiled at her and told her to sleep. The way he reminded her who she was—for herself, not for what she could do for others.

It had even got used to the lack of sleep and a whiny baby who wouldn't take a bottle and the terrible nappies and the ridiculously huge and old-fashioned pram.

She'd known this couldn't last for ever—or even for more than a week or so. So how had her heart grown so attached in so little time?

Was it just that this—this life with Willow and Max—was another thing she was being told she had to walk away from? Was that why it hurt so much?

'Wait and see what Janice has to say,' Max

said gently. 'My mother always used to say there was no point borrowing trouble—not when I already caused so much anyway.'

He'd said it to make her laugh, she knew, but all she could manage was a small smile.

Would he go back to London when Willow was gone? He'd hinted as much on several occasions. She'd hoped she would be able to help him integrate into the community here, in a way he never had as a child, but now it seemed as if she was out of time. He'd go, and visit for holidays or parties or whatever, and the Manor House would be just another holiday home—albeit a huge one—like so many of the picturesque cottages around the village.

It all seemed such a waste.

'Hopefully it's good news,' she said, forcing some cheer into her voice. 'If they've found Willow's family, and social services are happy to work with them, it could be a happy ending for everybody.'

'Just like you wanted,' Max reminded her.

'Just like I wanted.'

So why did she feel as if it was going to break her heart?

CHAPTER ELEVEN

'IT WAS ACTUALLY Terri Jacobs at the school who found her.' Janice was settled on the sofa in the study, with Lena beside her, while Max sat in his desk chair. The social worker, Sarah, was on a kitchen chair Lena had dragged in for her, and Willow bobbed happily in the Chair of Joy on the floor beside them.

He'd thought that the study sitting room would be cosier, more friendly than the larger drawing room with its borrowed furniture and baby equipment. But now it just felt as if the walls were closing in.

'She was a student, then?' Lena asked.

Max watched her as she spoke, noting the tension lines around her eyes, the way her hands were clasped tight in her lap. And, most of all, the way her gaze kept darting to Willow, then back to Janice.

It never landed on him, so she couldn't know how closely he was observing her. Checking for cracks in the calm, smiling, sensible exterior she always showed to people of the village.

There weren't any. Not that anyone else would notice. But Max had got very good at watching Lena Phillips over the last week.

'A fifteen-year-old,' Janice confirmed. 'She was terrified. She hid the pregnancy for the whole nine months, then went to stay with an older cousin a few towns away for the first couple of weeks of the summer holidays. Had the baby there, and didn't know what to do. When she came back…she was too scared to tell her parents, and she panicked.'

'But why leave Willow on *my* doorstep. And with that note?' It was the note, more than anything, that made no sense to Max. Why try to claim he was the father?

Sarah gave him a sympathetic smile. 'It appears that people around here have been talking a lot about you since word came you were moving into the Manor House.'

'So?' Max still didn't understand.

Lena made a small noise in the back of her throat, and shifted beside him on the sofa. 'I think I get it.'

He turned to look at her. 'Care to explain it to the idiot at the back of the class?'

She gave him a fond smile. 'For months, people have been talking about how rich you are, how handsome, your reputation with women.' She waggled her eyebrows at that. 'Honestly, they were mostly making it all up, I'm sure, but by the time you arrived half the village was convinced you were some rich playboy who slept with a dozen different women a week.'

'She thought I was promiscuous enough that I might believe I actually *was* the father?'

'Didn't you?' Sarah asked, eyebrows raised, and Max remembered, too late, their little white lie.

'I thought it was unlikely,' he said diplomatically. 'But of course I wanted to check with any women I might have been involved with before I could say definitively.'

Sarah looked amused, if disbelieving, so at least it didn't seem as if she was about to try and get him arrested for something.

'It wasn't just that, though,' Janice put in. 'I mean, look at this place.'

Max eyed the dark, gloomy study, and totally failed to see her point.

'Nobody who lived here could be short of money,' Lena explained. 'I imagine that Willow's mother hoped that you would be able to give her daughter a better life than she could hope to.'

'Not to mention the whole "lord of the manor" thing,' Sarah added. 'I mean, I grew up in Wishcliffe, and I know that whenever a family is in trouble there the first place they go is still Wishcliffe House, even in these modern times.'

'And Toby always helps,' Max said. It wasn't a guess, so much as a certainty he felt, deep inside. 'Willow's mother hoped I'd do the same.' Sarah nodded.

It all made a peculiar kind of sense, viewed through the lens of the village of Wells-on-Water. And it made him think of the place, and Lena's part in it, differently, too.

'Are you going to take her home now?' Lena asked.

'Willow's grandmother and grandfather have been told everything—by their daughter—and are, well, a bit shocked, I think, but determined to help. Willow's mother won't be alone with her baby any more; she has her family on her side and I think, between them and some help and support from us and the community, they're going to do okay.' Sarah smiled as she said it. Max supposed this had to be the best possible outcome for her.

'And Willow's mother won't be in any trouble?' He wasn't completely sure how he felt about that.

'She's going to get the help and support she needs for herself, as well as the baby,' Janice said. 'I don't think it's in anyone's interest—least of all Willow's—to punish her. Do you?'

'No,' Max said. 'No, of course not.'

'Can we…will we get to meet her?' Lena's voice wavered just a little and Max knew what she was really asking was 'will we see Willow again?' Because that was what his heart was asking, too.

'Right now the focus is just on helping them adjust,' Sarah said kindly. 'They did ask us to thank you, though. And to say sorry.'

'We didn't do it for the thanks.' Max got to his feet. If they were going, they might as well get moving now. No point in drawing out the goodbyes.

It didn't take long to put together the essentials Willow needed.

'There's a lot of stuff here people lent us to get started,' Lena said. 'I'm sure most of them would be happy to pass it on to Willow's family to help them, too. I'll check, and maybe you can arrange to get it to them?'

'I'm sure they'd be very grateful,' Sarah said.

'But she has to take the Chair of Joy now,' Max put in. 'It's her favourite. And Toby lent me a sling she really likes…'

Strange how his whole life had been taken over by such a small person. One who could change everything in just one short week.

Even stranger to imagine things going back to normal again tomorrow. To an empty house, and an empty heart.

Finally, it was time to say goodbye. He gave Willow a last cuddle, pressed a kiss against her downy hair, and made a promise he hoped nobody else could hear. He passed the baby to Lena, and purposefully didn't listen to whatever it was she whispered to her. Those words were private, like his.

And then they were gone, and the house echoed with the final closing of the door.

But Lena was still there, amazingly.

He looked at her, forced a smile. 'Do you want, I don't know, wine? Supper? Something?'

She gazed back at him for a long moment. Then she said, 'You,' and kissed him.

What am I doing?

Lena wasn't sure she knew the answer to her own question, but she did know she didn't want to stop. Kissing Max, touching Max, feeling his arms come up around her and hold her close… she didn't want the feelings that brought out in her to end.

She didn't want to stop and think. She just wanted to feel, for a change.

And it wasn't as if Max were complaining. He'd hauled her so tight against his body that she could feel *exactly* how much he didn't mind, and he groaned into her mouth as he deepened the kiss, turning them so he could press her up against the door Willow had just left through.

Not thinking about that.

'Are you sure?' He broke the kiss for a moment to ask, pulling back to gaze into her eyes. She wondered if her pupils were as blown with want as his were. 'We never got to that "later" talk.'

She shook her head and reached for him again. 'We don't need it. Not for this.'

Maybe later never needed to come. Maybe she could just have this, have him, for tonight.

Lose herself in him and worry about all the rest tomorrow.

That was all she wanted for now.

And it seemed Max was happy to go along with it.

They couldn't bring themselves to break apart as they headed for the stairs, which made navigating them a little tricky. Lena bashed her hip against the banister as they went, but she refused to stop and let Max check it. 'Upstairs,' she told him. 'Now.'

His room looked empty without the Moses basket in the corner, so she shut her eyes and pulled him down on top of her on the bed. When she opened them again, all she could see was him—and that was all she wanted to see.

Smiling at last, she began unbuttoning his shirt, stripping it from his shoulders even as he reached down to pull her top up over her breasts, then off completely.

Lena ran her hands down the firm planes of his chest. 'I was right. You did grow up well.'

Max gave a low chuckle in return. 'I'm not the only one,' he told her, then dropped his mouth to her breast, suckling the nipple through the fabric of her bra. 'I'm thinking this will all be a bit different from last time.'

'I should hope so.' She arched her back, her body desperate for more of his touch. 'We've had sixteen years to get better at it.'

'That's not what I meant.'

But before she could ask what he *did* mean, he had slid her skirt over her hips and down her thighs, following its path with his lips. Then, as she kicked the fabric away, he settled between her legs, shot her a knowing smile, and got to work.

It didn't take Lena very long to decide that this was *much* better than last time.

Max woke, stretched out an arm, and realised he was alone in the room.

The bed was cold. No Lena.

And no Moses basket in the corner. No Willow.

He sat up slowly, processing all the events of

the night before. From the unexpected ache at handing Willow over to be returned to her family, to the even less expected bliss he'd found in Lena's arms.

They'd needed each other last night. He'd known they should talk first, but in the moment... they'd needed each other, and that was enough. Touch, affection, distraction, pleasure...maybe it wasn't the best way for them to deal with their shared loss, but it had felt right in the moment.

Now, though, he wondered. As pleasurable as last night had been, had it been the wrong move? Otherwise, why wasn't he waking up with Lena beside him for another round?

Maybe she'd just gone to get coffee, he thought, but his optimistic side was still a work in progress, so he didn't really believe it. He listened out all the same for the sound of her footsteps on the stairs, or her singing in the kitchen.

He frowned. There were voices downstairs, but they weren't Lena's. And the footsteps he heard were too heavy to be hers.

Swinging his legs out of bed, he began to hunt for his clothes, pulling them on quickly before going to investigate.

Downstairs, it was a reversal of the first night Lena had stayed over, the morning after they found Willow. Once again, half of the village seemed to be in his home—but rather than bringing furniture and baby stuff, this time they were taking it away.

'What's happening?' he asked Janice, sleepily, when he found her directing operations at the bottom of the stairs.

'Lena called around first thing, asked people to either come and collect their stuff, or donate it to Willow's family,' she explained. 'Hugh Francis, the plumber, brought his van so we can drive things around. Most people are loading their stuff directly into it to donate.'

Of course Lena had found a way to keep helping Willow, even after she was gone from their lives; Max wasn't even surprised.

But he did want to talk to her. One topic of their 'later' discussion really did need to become more of a 'now' talk, he felt.

'Where *is* Lena?'

Janice's smile turned a little awkward, and he instantly began to worry how much Lena had said to her friend about what had happened after she left the night before.

'She had to go,' the doctor said. 'One of her brothers called from The Fox. Said they needed her for a family meeting.'

Because that didn't sound ominous or anything.

'Do you think you can handle everything here?' he asked.

Janice nodded. ‘Yeah. No problems. Anything you want me to make sure they don’t take?’

‘The coffee maker,’ Max called back over his shoulder, already halfway out of the door.

He needed to talk to Lena. And if she was at The Fox with her brothers…well, that was where he was going, too.

CHAPTER TWELVE

LENA SIGHED AS she stared down at the paperwork her brothers had laid out for her along the bar.

'I just don't understand how you let things get this bad.'

'Right, because this is all *our* fault,' Gary said over the top of his pint glass. 'Where were *you* when the bank started demanding money?'

Earning a living somewhere else because you wouldn't let me do it here.

She sighed again. Reason had no hope with Gary and Keith. But something in her told her she had to try anyway. 'Dad left the pub to the two of you,' she pointed out. 'Not me.'

'So you punished us by not helping.' Keith tossed another dart at the board on the far wall. 'Just like you always managed to blame us for everything, so you could swoop in and save the day.'

'Saviour complex, that's what Daisy says you have,' Gary added.

Daisy, as far as Lena was aware, got all of her psychological insights from other people's social media rants, rather than any sort of formal training. Lena had also never seen her less than tipsy, and usually a lot further into drunk. She'd been a great drinking pal of her father in his later years, but never much of a fan of Lena.

'And does Daisy also have any suggestions of how to get you out of this mess?' Lena asked, gesturing towards the stacks of paper that all told the same story. Gary and Keith both looked away without answering, which Lena supposed was answer enough.

The Fox had never been a massively lucrative business, but it did well enough to keep going, and, since they all lived on site in the sizeable flat above the bar, they hadn't needed much more than that.

But in the two years since their father had passed away, it seemed that the boys' needs had become greater—or perhaps just that the time dedicated to the pub had dipped even lower. Because they weren't even breaking even now. They were haemorrhaging money every month, and it was fair to say that the bank had noticed. They needed to fix things—fast—if they wanted to hold onto the pub at all.

So of course they had called her for help. Because this was what she did, wasn't it?

All their lives she'd fixed their mistakes, she'd cleaned up after them, made apologies on their behalf, and stopped them doing some truly stupid things.

Maybe Daisy was right. Maybe she *did* have a saviour complex. What else explained moving in with Max Blythe for a whole week, giving her heart to a baby she *knew* wouldn't be staying and—worse—to a man she knew wouldn't, either.

Max had all but said the same when they went out for dinner, that she did everything for others, but never stopped to think about what she needed to do, or wanted to do, for herself. The last time she had…it had been the day after she lost her virginity to Max.

And here she was, with history repeating itself.

What was she going to choose? To help save her family pub—and her brothers—from ruin, or to walk away and seek her own path? It frightened her to realise that she really wasn't sure.

Before she had to make a decision, though, the pub door opened—and Max Blythe strolled in.

'Well, if it isn't the prodigal son returned,' Gary said, with a snide smile. 'I heard they killed the fatted calf for you.'

'*I* heard they gave up their firstborn,' Keith countered. 'Or was it *your* firstborn? Depends who you listen to, I guess.'

Lena's chest tightened at her brother's words, but Max ignored them both, heading straight for her. Frowning down at her with concern, he took her hands in his. 'Everything okay here? Janice said there was some sort of emergency.'

Lena tugged her hands from his grip and stepped back. Max had been gone a long time, but the village had long memories—and he'd humiliated her brothers, once, before leaving. They wouldn't have forgotten.

Not to mention all the rumours swirling around the village about him—not just about him being Willow's father, but about the fortune he'd made before he came home. The last thing she needed was her brothers deciding that she was a way into Max's money, if they realised how close they were.

But she was too slow, or her brothers were too quick. They'd never been stupid men, just lazy ones, and they'd seen whatever flickered between her and Max and the possibilities it held instantly.

'So now you're back, I imagine you're looking to right past wrongs, huh, Max? Or do we have to call you "Milord" now?' Gary stepped out from behind the bar, closer towards them.

Lena wrapped her arms around her middle and tried to think of a way out of this. She could see the whole scene unfolding before her, and she just couldn't see a way to stop it.

'I don't have a title,' Max replied, his voice tight. 'Nor any past wrongs to make up for, as far as I'm aware.'

Gary and Keith shared a look at that. 'Really? I imagine our little Lena feels differently, don't you?'

'Keith, stop it.' They ignored her, as always.

'What do you mean?' Max asked, his eyes on her, not her brothers.

'Why, leaving her here. Alone. Pregnant.' Gary articulated the word so clearly it hung in the air between them, a ghost of a time she'd hoped she'd left behind.

And there it was. The memory she'd been trying her hardest to suppress since he'd returned.

They'd been there, that night, at the river. It wasn't as if there was much else to do in a village like Wells-on-Water. And even if no one else had noticed her sloping off with Max, her brothers had.

Max's face had drained of colour, his eyes heavy with confusion. 'You said—' He broke off, obviously remembering what she *had* said.

That he'd never called to check. That he'd left

without thinking about it. Leaving any consequences for her to deal with. She'd said it was fine.

That bit had been a lie.

And okay, she'd lied a little bit more when they'd gone out for dinner and she'd told him that it was just spending that one night talking with him that had changed her mind about leaving the village. The positive pregnancy test had had a lot to do with it, too. She hadn't had a clue what to do, but she'd known she couldn't do it in Wells-on-Water.

This was the conversation she'd known they had to have later. The one she'd been hoping she could postpone as long as possible.

'So you can see why we think you might have some reparations to pay, mate,' Keith said. 'And as it happens, the pub here could do with a little help. I'm sure Lena would consider the debt paid if—'

That was the breaking point. The one she'd felt coming—felt her whole existence starting to crack—but not quite known when it would hit.

With a last look at Max, Lena turned and walked out.

She couldn't take it a moment longer. She'd dealt with this her whole life. She'd been the convenient, reliable sister who took care of trouble, who fixed problems—first for her family, and now for the whole damn village.

And when she'd had a problem…a real one, a baby growing inside her, a family who'd shun her rather than support her, and no way to contact the father…she'd run, because she'd known she'd be on her own.

Now, she hoped, things would be different. But back then, it had seemed like the only choice.

She hadn't even known that her brothers had found out, until she'd come home for Christmas, months later. Gary had looked her up and down, taken in her flat belly, and shared one of those horrible, knowing looks with Keith.

'Took care of it, did you?' he'd said. *'Good girl. Last thing we need around here is another mouth to feed.'*

She supposed they'd found the test in her bedroom bin, and cursed herself for not being more careful. But it wasn't as if anyone else ever *emptied* the bins, so she'd assumed she'd be safe.

But her brothers loved knowledge that they could hold over others. She shouldn't have been surprised that they'd searched her room. And at least it had explained why they hadn't kicked up as much of a fuss as Dad about her leaving; they'd known why she had to go.

Heaving deep breaths, she stopped, just a

short walk away, opposite the crumpled shell of the village hall. She leaned against the low stone wall outside the shops, gripping the cold stone so tightly her hands felt numb, and stared at the collapse of her best efforts to help this damn village.

She'd never wanted another girl to feel the way she had felt, staring at that pregnancy test. As if there was nowhere to turn, and nowhere to go. She'd worked her whole adult life, since returning to Wells-on-Water, to try and make it the sort of place where people supported each other, no matter what they were going through. Somewhere where *everyone* had a place to go, when they needed it.

But she'd failed. Otherwise Willow's mother would never have felt as if she had to abandon her baby on the doorstep of a man temperamentally unsuited to taking her in. The fact that Lena had been there had been pure chance, a fluke.

One last chance for her to try and do good.

And maybe she had, for that one baby. But what had really changed?

The next time some poor girl felt that desperate, Lena might not be there. And what then?

She couldn't fix every problem on her own, and, to be honest, she didn't even want to.

Max would be leaving for London again

soon—maybe he'd already gone, now her brothers had outed her secret. He wasn't likely to forgive her for keeping that from him in a hurry. She'd screwed up, and that wasn't allowed. Growing up in Wells-on-Water had made that very clear to her.

She'd lost Willow, Max, the comfortable familiarity of the Manor House—not to mention her job, and now it looked like the family pub, too.

Where did she go from here?

Lena had no idea. So she just started walking, and hoped she'd figure it out.

Max looked up at the facade of Wishcliffe House and, not for the first time, imagined what it might have been like to grow up there, with his half-brothers. A pointless fantasy, especially after so many years, but one he'd never quite been able to shake.

And now, it was coloured by another daydream. What might have been if Lena had found him, sixteen years ago, and told him the truth.

Had she terminated the pregnancy? Or given the baby up for adoption? Perhaps even left it on a doorstep somewhere, like Willow. Her brothers hadn't known—or seemed to much care, beyond the fact that it hadn't been a drain on their finances.

But Max cared.

He'd searched for Lena, once he'd escaped her brothers' grasping clutches, but she was nowhere to be seen. By the time he'd made it back to the Manor House Janice was just finishing packing up, and confirmed that Lena hadn't been back there, either.

They needed to talk. But as the man who'd walked away from her when it turned out she had really needed him, even if he hadn't known that, he didn't feel as if he could chase or hound her now. She'd come to him when she was ready, he hoped.

And finally they'd have that 'later' talk, even if it wouldn't look anything like the one he'd imagined a day ago.

Climbing the front steps to Wishcliffe House, Max prepared to knock—only for the door to swing open before he even reached it.

'You're here!' Toby beamed at him with a manic gleam in his eyes, somewhere between utter joy and pride, and the complete devastation that came from not sleeping in a few days. 'Come and meet your nephew.'

His nephew. Not his half-nephew, or sort of relation. Toby had embraced him as a new brother whether Max liked it or not—and to his surprise, Max found that he did.

He couldn't go back to London until he'd met

his new baby nephew, and so Max had stayed a few more days. He kidded himself that the delay had nothing to do with hoping that Lena might show up.

Toby ushered him through the house, the rooms dimmed by half-closed shades, through to a cosy sitting room where Autumn was installed on a padded rocking chair, a tiny bundle in her arms. She smiled tiredly as Max approached.

'Benjy's first visitor,' she said. 'I'm so glad it's you.'

'Finn and Victoria will be by later, too,' Toby added. 'Then he'll have met the whole family.'

'You called him Benjamin?' Max reached out a finger into the bundle, crouching beside the chair. A tiny hand wrapped around it, and he felt his heart melt.

'Benjamin Harry Blythe,' Toby said. 'We were hoping you might agree to stand up as his godfather?'

'I'd be honoured.' He already knew he'd do anything for this tiny scrap of a human, the same way he would have for Willow, if needed.

As he hoped he would have for his and Lena's child, if he'd known.

A week ago, he'd arrived in Wells-on-Water with no interest in babies, or family, or settling down—and certainly not looking for love. The kind of domesticity Autumn and Toby had here—the kind he'd shared with Lena and Willow—would have made him shudder and step away in disgust.

Or maybe in fear. Because he hadn't known how this sort of life was supposed to work. It wasn't something he'd had before, or even really seen modelled for him.

But now he'd experienced it, even by accident… Max knew he couldn't be fully happy in this world without having it again. It might not have been what he'd ever have thought he wanted, but it turned out it *was* what he needed.

He just had to hope he might find it again. One day. The real thing, rather than a sham of a family set-up as he'd been acting out with Lena this week.

And maybe this time, he'd get to keep it.

The housekeeper, Mrs Heath, brought tea and biscuits, and Max settled down on the sofa to share all the small tricks he'd learned for coping with life with a newborn over the last week. Autumn and Toby soaked them all up, which surprised him.

'You probably know all this already from the books,' he said, after a while, embarrassed to have been going on so long. He knew Autumn had put together a veritable library of baby books over the last six months.

'You'd be surprised,' she said wryly. 'So many of them focus on what happens during pregnancy, or birth—but not so much on what happens afterwards.'

'And even the ones that do aren't much help,' Toby added. 'Benjy doesn't seem to be the sort to conform to what a book says he should be doing.'

'I wonder where he gets that from,' Max said mildly, pointedly not looking directly at either of Benjamin's parents.

'But what about you?' Autumn asked. 'We heard that they found Willow's mother, and her family are supporting her. That's good news, isn't it?'

Max nodded. 'The best we could have hoped for, really.' Even if it had bruised his heart a little. And losing Willow *and* Lena in the same twenty-four hours…

He reached for another biscuit.

'I bet the Manor House feels kind of quiet and empty now,' Autumn said. 'Unless Lena is still staying with you…'

Toby laughed. 'You don't have to answer that, Max. My wife has a terrible habit of fishing for gossip—even, it seems, after a very long couple of days here.'

Autumn rolled her eyes. 'Like you weren't wondering the exact same thing.'

'But *I* didn't ask it.'

'Because you knew that I would.'

Max decided to stop this argument in its tracks before what would usually be flirtatious banter between the two of them became something serious through sleep deprivation.

'Lena isn't there. I don't know where she is, actually,' he admitted. 'She…left. The day after Willow went home. Janice says she's not at her cottage, and she hasn't been back to The Fox, either.' He'd checked, reluctantly, when there'd been no sign of her for a full twenty-four hours.

Toby and Autumn exchanged a look.

'Tell us what happened,' Toby said.

'We can help,' Autumn added. 'And you can have a cuddle with Benjy. That will help.'

Max had never been one for sharing his feelings, let alone airing his relationship problems. But somehow, with his brother and sister-in-law listening with concerned faces, and the warmth of a newborn baby in his arms, telling them everything seemed like the most natural thing in the world.

So he did.

Everything. Starting sixteen years ago and bringing them right up to the moment that Lena slammed out of the pub without looking back.

He looked up at the end to find them both

watching him with wide eyes, and all the biscuits gone.

'So?' he asked. 'What do I do now?'

They exchanged another one of those wordless looks that seemed to contain whole paragraphs.

'Just to be clear,' Autumn said. 'You do realise that you're in love with Lena, right?'

Max blinked. Love? He hadn't thought about love. Because everything they'd shared that week had only been pretend. A convenience, for Willow and her mother's sake, rather than theirs.

Not love. He just…needed to know she was okay. To help her. To be with her and support her in whatever she wanted to do next. To come home to her every night and talk about their days. To have her support in chasing his dreams, too. To work together towards shared dreams, come to that. To kiss her and hold her and make love to her again as they had that last night. And maybe to one day share again what they'd had with Willow with their own baby…

Oh.

Right.

'Of course I realise that,' he said, not feeling it was necessary to point out that the revelation was only a few seconds old. 'The question is, what do I do about it?'

* * *

Lena hadn't told anyone that she was coming back to Wells-on-Water to clear out her cottage and hand the keys back to the landlord. She hadn't wanted a welcoming committee on the doorstep, or even her brothers coming to hound her for money, or anything else. She'd known that her return—and her absence, for that matter—probably wouldn't have gone unnoticed. But still, she'd hoped she'd be able to get in and out in the minimal possible time, and without any drama.

Her hopes started to fade when she drove past Mrs Jenkins, standing outside her shop with her hands on her hips, watching her. Lena raised a hand to wave, but Hillary had already turned and gone back inside.

Lena sighed. Looked as if people were mad with her for leaving. She could understand that. They'd got used to having her around, fixing problems, getting involved. Keeping the wheels of the village turning.

She'd got used to it, too. She missed it. But she knew she had to think about what *she* wanted from life, as well as what others needed. It had taken her a lot of years to learn the lesson, but now she was there, she couldn't risk backsliding.

She still wanted to help, though. That was why she'd been applying for a different sort of job, from her room in her temporary rental in the capital. Fund-raising jobs, assistant roles at charities, that sort of thing. She'd hoped that her experience in hospitality would help her get a foot in the door, but it seemed that these roles were harder fought for than she'd expected—and she was older than the average candidate, straight out of university.

One recruitment agency she'd spoken to had told her, rather bluntly, that she was the worst of both worlds. Over-qualified and under-experienced for the roles she was applying for.

But Lena had faith that she'd find the right thing. An opening where she could, finally, really make the difference she'd been craving in the world, without the possibility of having it snatched away from her again at any moment. *That*, she'd decided, was what mattered most to her.

And if she was focussing her search in London, well, that was just common sense. Lots of charitable organisations headquartered there, after all. The chance that she might bump into Max again—by accident or design—when she was ready, and prepared to face what had gone between them in the past and perhaps move on to something that could be between them in the future, total coincidence.

That was what she told herself, anyway.

The only problem was, she admitted to herself as she drove through the village towards her cottage, she missed Wells-on-Water. She missed the community, the people, the shops, the sea nearby and the big skies above. She missed making a visible difference, rather than an anonymous one. She missed even the chance of seeing Willow thriving with her real family.

And she missed Max, most of all. Much as her brain tried to deny it, her heart was very clear on the matter.

She passed the church, Roberto's restaurant, the craft shop, The Fox. And at each location, anyone outside enjoying the sunshine disappeared inside the moment she appeared.

Clearly she really was persona non grata. The thought hurt, but at least it would make it easier to leave again.

Her cottage was much as she had left it, when she reached it. Although she'd been renting it for several years now, it had never *quite* felt like home, not least because the landlord wouldn't let her decorate or do anything to soften the edges of the stark, clean white look he'd gone for.

Lena pulled two large suitcases from under her bed, and set about packing up her worldly belongings, ready for her next adventure, wishing she could feel a little more excited about it.

Maybe a cup of tea would help with that.

She'd just made her way downstairs to click on the kettle, when the front door crashed open behind her, and Lena spun to find Max standing in the doorway, his face shadowed by the sun from behind him, but his chest moving with deep, heaving breaths.

She blinked. 'How did you know I was here?'

'Are you kidding?' Max gave a low laugh. 'Every single person you drove past on your way into the village called me to tell me.' The phone in his hand began to buzz, and he checked the screen. 'That's your brothers, about fifteen minutes behind the curve, as usual.' He declined the call.

'Gary and Keith phoned you?' This made no sense at all. 'Why would *anyone* call you? And why are you even still here in Wells-on-Water? Weren't you going back to London?'

And why was he just standing there? Had he really waited here for her to yell at her for lying about the baby, all those years ago? Could he be that furious, still? Oh, she'd really wanted to put a bit of distance between them and that awful last scene at The Fox before she saw him again. She'd wanted to be a success, as he'd become, to meet him as an equal this time.

But here he was. And God help her, Lena wasn't going to send him away. And she wasn't going to run, either. Not this time.

It was time to face this—face him, face her future—head-on. And she was ready.

'Max,' she said, when he just stared at her rather than answering any of her very reasonable questions. 'Why are you here?'

CHAPTER THIRTEEN

MAX SHOOK HIMSELF out of the trance that seemed to have come over him on seeing her again, and searched for the right answer. The one that would make things right between them. That would explain to her how much this meant to him—but not scare her away at the same time. The one that would get him the answers *he* needed, too.

'Can I come in?' he asked. 'This might take a bit of explaining, and I'm half expecting an audience of locals out there at any minute.'

'It wouldn't surprise me.' Lena watched him, warily. 'Okay, since you don't seem about to yell at me, you can come in.'

Max shut the door quietly behind him. 'Why would I yell at you?'

'For lying about the consequences of what happened sixteen years ago.' She dropped down to sit on the edge of the white sofa, looking uncomfortable. 'For running away when you found out.'

He glanced around the strangely white and

impersonal lounge, and took a seat on the chair opposite her, deciding quickly it was the most uncomfortable chair he'd ever sat on.

'I ran away first,' he said carefully. 'Do I wish I'd known the truth? Yes. But I wasn't there, and I hadn't left you any way to find me. And while I hope you will tell me what happened, it's your story to share when you're ready.'

'I lost the baby.' The words blurted out of her, and Max felt his heart break and mend at the same time. Break, because it had been his child, and because she'd had to go through that all alone. Mend, because she'd trusted him enough to tell him the truth.

'I'm so sorry.' He wanted to reach out and take her hand. No, he wanted to fold her into his arms and keep her there. But he couldn't push her. He needed to listen, first.

'It was my first week at university. Everyone else was out partying for Freshers' Week, and I…well. Wasn't.' She'd been dealing with a miscarriage instead. Alone.

'I wish I'd known. I wish I'd been there with you.' He looked down at his hands, shaking his head. 'I wish I hadn't been such an idiot eighteen-year-old to walk out on you as if there was no chance of consequences.'

'I wished that, too.' Lena gave him a lopsided smile. 'But now…these are the experiences that made us who we are. There's no going backwards.'

'Was that why…I mean, part of it anyway… why you were so determined to find Willow's mum and help her? To look after Willow until she was found?'

Lena nodded. 'I think so. I just kept imagining if it had been me, if I'd been the one stuck in this village, scared and alone. I'd worked so hard for years to help the people around here, to give them a place to go when they had nowhere else, to help and support them. And a lot of that was because *I* didn't have that, when I needed it. When my mum died, people had rallied around—because that wasn't her fault, and I was young and alone, and I apologised for my brothers and my father and I tried hard. Because I was a good girl, and I did what they thought were the right things. But they wouldn't think that any more. I'd seen how they treated you… because of something that wasn't even your fault. Nobody shamed your father for sleeping with your mum and getting her pregnant. They shamed her for telling the truth about it.'

He wished he could tell her she was wrong, but he knew she wasn't. 'So you left. And then you came back and *changed things*. Lena, do you even know how amazing that is?'

She shook her head. 'I tried. I don't know if I succeeded.'

'I do. Willow and her mum and her family do. Everyone you've helped does.' He reached out now, and she met him halfway, her fingers intertwining with his in a way that made his heart leap with hope. 'Wells-on-Water isn't the place it was when I grew up, and that's thanks to you. Now, if someone needs help, they're not shamed for it. They *get* it. That's incredible.' And he wanted to help her keep doing that work. But only if that was what she wanted, too.

Lena pulled her hands from his. 'I went to London, you know.'

'London? Why?' It was hard to imagine her so far from home, alone. Wells-on-Water had always been part of who Lena was. He hated to think that anything he had done could have taken that from her.

But as he listened to her explaining about her job search in the capital, what she was trying to do there, he knew that nothing had really changed, not at heart.

As she finished he took a breath, and tried to figure out his next move.

'What?' she asked, frowning. 'What's the matter?'

'I'm trying to figure out how to say something.'

She rolled her eyes. 'Then just say it, idiot. Do you really think there's *anything* we can't admit to each other at this point? You've known me since birth; we watched each other grow up. You've seen me naked—at eighteen and thirty-four. We've discussed our mistakes, our pasts—hell, we've even co-parented for a week. What can you possibly need to say to me that's so scary compared to all of that?'

'I'm in love with you.'

Lena stared at him, her mind a sudden and complete blank. 'What?'

She could see him swallow before he responded. 'You asked me why I came here. Why I'm still in Wells-on-Water. Why everyone called me to tell me you were here. And you asked me what was so scary I almost couldn't say it. And the answer to all of those questions is the same thing: I'm in love with you.'

She needed to reply. She needed to say something, but there were no words left in Lena's head.

'I knew it the moment you left,' Max went on, then winced. 'Okay, not quite the same moment. But it didn't take me long. I realised that, while I missed Willow, what was really breaking my heart was not seeing you every day. Not coming home to you. Not talking about our days. Not being able to help you in your non-stop campaign to make the world a better, kinder place. And I didn't know where you'd gone, but I knew you'd have to come back here eventually. So I went around the village and I told everyone.'

'You told them you were in love with me?'

He smiled. 'No. I wanted to save that for you. But to be honest, I think they probably all knew before I did. I just told them that I needed to talk to you, and if they saw you they should ring me.'

'And they did. All of them.' All those friends and acquaintances who'd disappeared inside when they saw her. They hadn't been shunning her. They'd been calling Max, so he could come here and tell her he loved her.

All those people who'd made life difficult for Max his whole childhood. He'd gone to them for help, and they'd given it.

Maybe she really had changed something, after all. And maybe part of that something was Max.

'All of them,' he echoed. 'Even Mrs Jenkins, who it seems loves you more than she hates me. Even your brothers. Who, by the way, have a new manager at the pub.'

'You gave them money?' she asked incredulously.

'No, I gave *your* family pub the expertise it needed to get it back on its feet. Her wages come out of the profits, and your brothers have to do what she says or she walks. I think they hate it.'

'I think I love it.' She frowned. 'You didn't think I might want to do that job?'

'Not really.'

'Because I was gone?'

'Because your heart wouldn't be in it.' Max tilted his head as he looked at her, a fond smile on his lips, and Lena felt her heart contract. 'You're a great manager, I have absolutely no doubt about that. But you studied hospitality because you wanted to help your family, not because it was what *you* wanted to do. And more than anything I want you to be able to choose what you *want* to do, not what you think others need, for once.'

'And you know what I want?' Because that was kind of presumptive.

He laughed. 'Hell, no. I mean, I have some ideas, but I'm waiting for you to tell me. And then I'll help you make it happen.'

'What?' None of this was making any sense.

Max shifted to the edge of his seat, reaching out to take her hands again. He gazed into her eyes, holding her attention completely as he spoke. 'I told you I love you. And that's new for me—loving someone else. But since I came home to Wells-on-Water, I think I've learned a bit about what it means. I've seen it with Toby and Autumn, with Finn and Victoria. And I've seen it most with Willow, and with you. The way you loved that baby and helped me love her, too. And the way you love this village, and all the people in it who adore you back, even if they're not great at showing it. You've all taught me. And this is what I've learned:

'Loving someone means supporting them, helping them towards their best lives, and their best selves. It means letting them go if that's what's best for them, and holding on tight if that's what they need. So I let you go when you needed to, and now you're back… I had to tell you I love you. And I'll do anything I can to support you, to help you do whatever it is you think you need to do next. It doesn't matter if you feel the same. Because my love for you? It's not about me. It's all about the incredible woman you are.'

Lena swallowed around the lump that had taken root in her throat and blinked her burning eyes. 'You have that much faith in me? Even if you don't think I love you back?'

'Yes,' he said simply. Then he dropped her hands and got to his feet. 'Which is why I'm going to go back to the Manor House now, and I'll be there when you figure out what you want your next move to be. You decide you want to save an endangered dung beetle in Outer Mongolia, I'll help you plan how and fund the expedition. You want to tell me I'm wrong about you wanting to run The Fox, I'll fire the new manager and put you in charge—hell, I'll buy the place from your brothers if that's what you need to feel fulfilled. Whatever it is, you know where I am.'

Lena jumped up as he turned and moved towards the door. 'And what if…?' She swallowed again as he paused, his back towards her. 'And what if what I need is you?'

Max felt his heart soar at her words, and he spun to face her so fast that the whole world seemed to tilt.

'What if what I need most in the world is to love you back?' Lena asked.

'Is it?' he whispered, barely daring to believe it.

She gave him a lopsided smile in return. 'Well, I could go for some of Roberto's chocolate pudding, too, but…yes. Max, why do you think I went to London?'

'For a job?'

'For *you*. Because I thought, after a while, maybe we could try again. Third time's the charm and all that. I figured you'd be going back there for work and, well, maybe we'd have a chance, away from all the history here.'

'But you *like* the history here. It's our history.'

'It is.' Stepping forward, she took his hand and tugged him closer, and he wrapped his other arm around her waist. 'I love this village.'

'I know,' Max said. 'And, actually, I've grown weirdly fond of it, too.'

'Good. Because I love you, too.'

His heart lightened at the words, as if the weight of years and years had just lifted away, and the world had opened up to another chance.

'So, you'll stay here? With me?'

'I already gave my landlord notice...'

'That works out nicely, then, because by "here" I meant the Manor House,' Max admitted, and she laughed.

'That could work,' Lena said. 'I will still need a job, though. I'm not good at sitting around doing nothing.'

'I'd never noticed,' he said drily, and she stuck her tongue out at him. 'I already told you. Name it, and I'll be here to support you.'

She bit down on her lower lip, chewing it as she thought. 'I think...I think I want what I've always wanted,' she said finally. 'To make this village the best it can be. So that nobody here ever needs to go hungry, or feel lonely, or be afraid and feel like they have nowhere to turn. People like Willow's mum, or you when you were a kid. I want them all to feel welcome. And I want to help them all.'

'You want to build a new community hub,' he guessed.

'A better one,' she corrected. 'With proper therapists and training courses and baby groups and a food bank and a creche and—'

'Everything Wells-on-Water needs,' he summarised, before she could get too carried away.

'Exactly.'

'Then that's what we'll do,' he promised. 'Together.'

'Together,' she echoed. 'I think that's my favourite part.'

'Mine, too,' he admitted as he kissed her.

She broke away suddenly. 'What about what you need?'

'If I've got you, that's all I need,' he said.

Lena rolled her eyes. 'That's marvellously romantic, but not true. What is it that *you* want to do with your life?'

Sensing she was serious, Max stepped back and thought. 'Well, I genuinely believe in what you want to do here, and I want to help you with it. I've already built my own business, had wild success…and I want to keep my hand in there, too, but I have good people on staff, so a lot of it I can do from here, most of the time. But I guess the one thing I really want is something

I've never had.' Swallowing, he met her gaze. 'A family. With you.'

Her eyes widened.

'I know, it's too much, too fast,' he hurried on. 'And I'm not saying now. But one day, when you're ready. That's what I want—what I dream of. Marrying you and having a family together. If that's what you want, too.'

Reaching up, she placed a hand on the side of his face and pressed a soft kiss to his lips. 'One day, probably not very long from now, knowing us, that's exactly what we'll have.'

And this time, when she kissed him, Max saw their whole lives together stretching out ahead of them. Filled with laughter and love, happiness and hard work, dreams and determination.

He couldn't wait for any of it.

EPILOGUE

THIS YEAR'S FIRE FESTIVAL seemed to burn brighter and more joyous than any previous year, Lena thought. Or perhaps that was just because she was happier than she'd been, ever before.

She tucked her arm through Max's and huddled against his side as they made their way around the field, checking out all the delights on offer.

At the sweet stall, there was a long queue of school children growing. Beside it, she saw that the mulled-wine tent was also doing a roaring trade—in fact, she could see Finn and Victoria sharing a mug beside their new daughter's pram.

Up on the stage, a folk duo was performing—a fast and fun tune that had people on their feet dancing. Lena squinted up at the stage, sure she recognised one of them, but unable to place him.

Amongst the dancers was Autumn, holding Benjy in her arms as she moved to the music, a swirl of colour in the firelight.

Lena glanced around for Max's brother, and found him holding court a little way away. Sitting on a wooden toadstool, Toby was surrounded by a group of entranced kids as he told them stories Lena suspected were rather more spooky than their parents would necessarily like.

'Ah, there they are,' Max said, and Lena glanced over to where he was pointing. Behind another stall, lit with fairy lights showing off the Wells-on-Water Community Hub logo, Kathy and Trevor were dealing with a small throng of people, all picking up leaflets and asking questions. 'Shall we say hi?'

As Lena watched, Kathy took down the details of a woman she recognised as a local businesswoman, hopefully volunteering, and Trevor handed one of their new fundraising packs to Dominic, the vicar.

'I think they've got things covered for now,' she said. 'And I want to go and get some of that hog roast before it's our turn to take a shift on the stall. Come on.'

They made their way around the huge bonfire at the centre of the field, heading for the hog roast.

There were plenty of families at the festival this year, Lena was pleased to see. But every buggy that went past, she still couldn't help but check if it might be Willow inside. Janice said she and her family were doing well, and that was all she could really hope for.

That and, maybe, a chance to do it all again with her own baby in the future.

She brought her hands together and twisted her engagement ring under her gloves. Maybe that future wouldn't be too far away.

And she couldn't wait to live every moment of it, here in her home village, with Max at her side.

* * * * *

If you enjoyed this story,
check out these other great reads
from Sophie Pembroke

Their Second Chance Miracle
Vegas Wedding to Forever
The Princess and the Rebel Billionaire
A Midnight Kiss to Seal the Deal

All available now!